KT-389-784

The Legend of
Keane O'Leary

When outlaw chief Keane O'Leary decides it's time to retire
from a life of banditry, he is unaware he is about to unleash a
bloody sequence of events that will make his past misdeeds
seem like a hillbilly shindig. His three daughters are the
inheritors of his empire of crime, and hell hath no fury like a
woman who covets her sisters' inheritance.

Brothers Alward and Monday Gallagher are caught up in
the vicious infighting unleashed by the retirement of the
bandit chief and the consequent rivalry of the sisters, and
have to wade through blood and bullets as mayhem ensues.
The arena soon becomes littered with the dead and dying
as the fateful sequence of events play out right up to the
blood-spattered finale.

The Legend of Keane O'Leary

P. McCormac

A Black Horse Western

ROBERT HALE

© P. McCormac 2018
First published in Great Britain 2018

ISBN 978-0-7198-2847-8

The Crowood Press
The Stable Block
Crowood Lane
Ramsbury
Marlborough
Wiltshire SN8 2HR

www.bhwesterns.com

Robert Hale is an imprint
of The Crowood Press

Typeset by
Derek Doyle & Associates, Shaw Heath
Printed and bound in Great Britain by
4Bind Ltd, Stevenage, SG1 2XT

1

Gallagher was seated in one corner of the saloon at a green baize table. This was where he normally conducted his business. Any outlaw wanting to operate within his domain did so only on paying a cut of his proceeds to the saloon owner. It was from here he bought stolen goods and sometimes financed forthcoming crooked deals. Gallagher raised his greying head when he heard the batwings swing open. From habit he touched the butt of the Navy Colt clipped to the underside of the table.

Three men slouched inside. Their sharp eyes searched the room like animals sizing up unfamiliar terrain. It was early in the day and there were not many customers in the saloon. A solitary bartender worked behind the bar, sorting bottles and glasses. Spotting Gallagher, the three men sauntered across towards him. From under lowered brows Gallagher sized up the trio.

That they were down on their luck was evident from their tattered clothing. All three were unshaven. Gallagher guessed they wouldn't have washed in a long time either. In spite of their down-at-heel appearance all three wore holstered pistols that looked well cared for. An uneasy feeling was growing in the saloon boss as the trio approached.

'You Gallagher?'

'Yep.'

The speaker, tall and thin with drooping moustache, hooked a saddle bag from his shoulder and dumped it on the table in front of Gallagher.

'Wore tole you might be interested in buying some quality goods.'

'Mebby. What you got?'

The man reached over and undid the strap of one wallet and emptied the contents onto the green baize. A collection of cheap jewellery and silverware tumbled onto the table.

Gallagher had seen such assortments before. These men were trash, preying on poor families travelling towards the gold fields of the West Coast. The paltry baubles lying on the table were tokens of misery. They were the gleanings of numerous hold-ups. In some cases there was blood on the booty. For men reduced to petty theft, making the shift to murder was just a step further down the slippery road to perdition.

'Five dollars,' Gallagher said.

The outlaws took a moment to digest this.

'Yore joshing, man. There's at least fifty dollars' worth there.'

'Not from where I'm sitting.'

'You thieving son of a bitch. There's three of us to divvy up. How about thirty?'

Gallagher sat relaxed but watchful. He was the town boss and founder of California Crossing – a motley collection of shacks and false-fronted buildings well removed from any civilized habitation.

California Crossing specialized in catering for the lawless breed. Bandits, cutthroats, rustlers, bank robbers and holdup men could find a haven among its brothels and saloons. Rustlers found a ready market for the beeves they stole. All brought their stolen wares and bartered for dollars, goods or drink or services.

No lawman would risk his life to take in the sights and sounds of California Crossing. For the law to brace the town would take an army of deputies and so far, that option had never been seriously considered by the law enforcement officers who operated within the vicinity of the outlaw town.

Gallagher raised his eyes and stared coldly at the men in front of him. He was aware the goods lying on the table were worth much more than the sum he offered. He was also aware of the unhappiness these men wreaked on impoverished travellers struggling to reach the promised gold diggings of California.

'Five, fellas, take it or leave it. I got cupboards bulging with this junk.'

'Son of a bitch, that's daylight robbery.' The words were spoken without any hint of irony. 'Fifteen. You know we'll spend it here anyways.'

Gallagher stared implacably back at the mean eyes glaring down at him.

'Can't do it, fella. I gotta living to make. Five's my best offer.'

Gallagher could see the signs – could see the anger and frustration building. He fumbled in a small drawer beneath the table and extracted a five-dollar bill. When he placed the note on the table his other hand remained out of sight. The spokesman for the trio stared at the money, nervously licking his lips.

'Come on. Yew can do better than that. I'll take fifteen. That's five each.' He turned to his companions. 'Hey, fellas? That'll do us, eh?'

The signal must have been passed then. All three palmed guns. The hidden Colt sent a slug into number one's leg. The heavy bullet broke his thigh and sent him stumbling and cursing back into his companions. As Gallagher unclipped the gun and was bringing it up to fire at the remaining triggermen there came an explosion from the direction of the bar. Lead shot flailed the gunmen. They yelled curses and although one got off a shot, it went somewhere into the ceiling.

Gallagher fired steadily at the two desperados. They staggered under the impact of the bullets – blood pumping from chest and belly wounds.

Gallagher's weapon clicked on empty and he fished around inside his jacket for the Colt in his shoulder holster. With the fresh gun in his hand he hesitated, watching cautiously. But the gunmen were on the floor, clutching ineffectually at blood spilling from the bullet holes stitched into their bodies. Gradually, as he watched, all movement ceased as the men succumbed to their wounds.

Slowly the saloon owner stood and walked around the table. The man who had been negotiating the sale lay in the sawdust, both hands clamped around his thigh, his pants leg soaked in dark blood.

'Son of a bitch, why'd the hell yew shoot? We woulda took the five.'

'Monday, get some help and get this scum across to the sawbones.'

The barkeep, a swarthy skinned youngster, came around the counter, still carrying the shotgun.

'Will I need this?' he asked.

'Nah. I guess we pulled their sting. Thanks, son. That was good work with the Greener.'

Gallagher turned back to the table and scooped the trinkets back into the saddle bag and handed it to the bartender.

'Take this with you. Tell Doc it's for patching up this scum. I'll keep bar until you come back.'

Recruiting help from among their patrons, the young barkeep gradually cleared the saloon of the dead and wounded. Muttering under his breath, Gallagher went behind the bar and poured a glass of bourbon. Gunplay always upset him and it would take a while for him to settle back into his normal routine.

Moodily he sipped at the drink, staring into space. The batwings creaked and drew his attention. He watched wryly as the hairiest human he had ever seen barrelled inside. With a sweeping glance, the newcomer took in the almost empty saloon then walked over to the bar. He rested both hands on the top and affected to read the bottles lining the shelves behind Gallagher's head.

Tangled iron-grey hair hung to below the man's shoulders. An equally unkempt beard sprouted from his face and hung to mid-chest. To enhance the hairy effect the man wore animal skins. A coonskin cap complete with tail perched atop his head. The sleeveless sheepskin jacket had seen better days and appeared to be moulting.

'Howdy, stranger,' Gallagher said, 'can I get you anything?'

'I'm looking for a drink that'll quench my thirst and still leave my tonsils in place.'

'Red Nugget whiskey should do the trick,' Gallagher said breezily. 'Smoothest drink this side of the Rockies.'

He plucked a bottle from a shelf and poured a measure into a glass.

'Try that.'

The newcomer put the drink to a gap in the beard and slurped noisily. When he put the empty glass down he sucked at the hair around his mouth then expelled his breath in a fierce gust.

'Umm. . . I've drunk mule's piss and it tasted better'n that poison,' he said speculatively. 'Better try another just to make sure it is whiskey and not piss.'

Gallagher's hand tightened on the whiskey bottle.

'Mister, if you don't like our drinks you can always try somewhere else.'

'I was told when I got to California Crossing to make sure

and call in and sample Gallagher's hospitality. I surely don't like your attitude. You go and get Gallagher down here. I want to make a complaint.'

'You son of a bitch, I am Gallagher. You can have that first drink on the house. Now turn around and go crawl into whatever rat hole you crawled outta.'

Any further conversation was interrupted by the return of Monday. The barkeep came behind the bar.

'OK, Pa. I can take over now,' the youngster said and then seeing the tension in Gallagher's face, glanced shrewdly at the bearded man. 'Everything all right?'

'Fine, son. This fella is just leaving.'

The stranger eyed up the barkeep. Monday was a handsome youth with a narrow face. The nose was long and straight above a slightly petulant mouth. The eyes were deep-set and there was a hint of arrogance quickly hidden when he saw the bearded man scrutinizing him.

'Sure, Pa,' the youth said, and awaited developments.

A broad grin split the bearded face of the stranger.

'Gallagher, you're sure one mean old galoot. What way's that to greet an old friend?'

Gallagher's eyes narrowed and he peered closely at the stranger.

'Old friend? I sure didn't know I had a monkey for a friend.'

'Monkey, my ass – Marcus Cogan, you old coot. You remember me – Marcus Cogan from the old days.'

'Well, I'll fart in a ten gallon hat. Marcus Cogan! You had me going then for a moment. Marcus Cogan! I was about to chuck you out in the street.' Gallagher slapped the bar. 'I'll be danged.' He poured from the bottle. 'Here, have another shot of piss.'

The whiskey disappeared into the hairy mouth. Cogan smacked his lips.

'Just kidding about the whiskey,' he said. 'It is good

stuff.' The hairy head nodded towards the barkeep. 'Did I hear right – he call you Pa?'

'Yeah, he's mine all right,' Gallagher replied. 'My very own kith and kin.'

'I didn't know you married a squaw.'

'Married! Hell, no. She was a whore as I took a fancy to. Right handsome female she was too. We had good times together afore she upped and went back to her people. Left me with Monday here. Called him that on account he was born on a Monday.

'Nah, I was married to a respectable gal – a preacher's daughter from Kansas. She gave me a right proper legit son, afore she went and died of fever. Alward's his name. He looks after the practical end of the business – warehousing, supplies, keeping the accounts and all that. Anyway, what brings you here to this neck of the woods?'

'O'Leary sent me.'

Gallagher placed his hands on the bar top and stared earnestly at Cogan.

'Keane O'Leary,' he said slowly. 'How is that old reprobate?'

'He's doing OK. Wants to throw a jamboree and he wants you to organize it.'

2

Gallagher ran two saloons, a dance hall and a couple of brothels. He decided the dance hall would be best suited to O'Leary's needs. In preparation for the function, he posted a notice cancelling Saturday night's fandango. This caused a bit of a stir among the dance hall patrons but the saloon owner ignored the protests and got on with the more important job of making sure O'Leary's function was a success.

'How many guests has O'Leary in mind?' he enquired of Cogan.

'Humph! You know Keane. He's liable to ask everyone he knows. My guess is about a hundred. You'd better lay in food and drink for that many at least.' The scout tossed a bag of gold dust at the town boss. 'O'Leary sent that as a down payment.'

Gallagher's two sons sat in on these discussions. Alward was delegated to organize the decoration of the hall as well as the entertainment. Monday got the task of stocking and running the bar and providing grub.

'O'Leary's developed a hankering after wine,' the bearded Cogan informed Monday. 'Better lay in plenty. Everyone'll want to drink what he drinks.'

Keane O'Leary was renowned in California Crossing. He was rather more infamous amongst the mine owners of the

Californian gold fields. The notorious bandit had created a climate of fear amongst the bankers and gold merchants. Somehow he seemed to know just when gold was being moved around. Shipments of bullion attracted O'Leary like a buzzard to a dead body. His raids were well planned and he hit only the large consignments.

After each successful attack he disappeared without trace until the next raid. His whereabouts during these lulls was a mystery. That his hideouts were effective was evident by the inability of the law to track him down and bring him to justice.

As soon as news of the coming celebrations leaked, and that O'Leary was coming to California Crossing, the citizens decided they were being honoured by the visit of such an eminent personage, albeit an outlaw and killer. Subsequently a delegation approached Gallagher and suggested a civic reception.

'Goddamn it,' Gallagher protested, 'it's a private function and only his friends are invited.'

'We just want to decorate the town some and have a holiday when he comes. He can't object to that. Goddamn it, we want to honour the Bandit King of the Californian Gold Fields.'

'All right, all right.' Gallagher threw up his hands in surrender. 'Do as you see fit.'

Keane O'Leary rode into California Crossing on a big sturdy roan. Ten of his men had ridden in earlier to make sure the town was safe pending his visit. O'Leary never left anything to chance. An outlaw town would attract bounty hunters on the lookout to make some reward money by roping in a man wanted by the law. The price on O'Leary's head was enough to set up a man for life.

Flags and bits of coloured cloth had been hung out in honour of his visit. The inhabitants of California Crossing

13

lined the sidewalks and called out greetings as the famous
bandit chief entered the town. O'Leary ignored the crowds,
staring straight ahead as he rode in with his entourage.

O'Leary was a lean built man. His face was the colour
and texture of dried rawhide. Deep lines of encroaching
age were etched into his hard face. His mouth was a straight
slash – the lips barely discernible in the texture of his
weather-beaten skin. Cold narrow eyes stared out beneath
sparse, grey eyebrows.

His daughters rode behind him. If the populace were
anxious to view the king they were doubly eager to see the
daughters of the king – the youngest was Catlin, the eldest
Gertrude and the middle daughter, Rachel.

Around O'Leary rode a bunch of hard-eyed gunmen. It
was said the bandit leader never travelled anywhere without
a bodyguard of at least ten men. Counting the men already
in the town and the main body of riders now riding in,
Cogan's estimate of one hundred guests was not far off the
mark. They rode straight to the dance hall where Gallagher
waited to greet him.

'Dang my hide, Gallagher, you're getting nearly as old as
myself.'

The two men shook hands warmly. They were old
friends. Gallagher had been one of the original members of
O'Leary's gang before branching out on his own. The old-
timers knew and trusted each other.

'Let's get this party rolling,' O'Leary said. 'I'm dry as a
buffalo chip.'

While O'Leary pushed inside, Gallagher courteously
waited to greet the O'Leary females. The only one of the
three that acknowledged him was Catlin. She smiled and
kissed him briefly on the cheek.

'How are you, Gallagher?' she asked him. 'You never
look any different no matter how long it is between seeing
you.'

'Miss Catlin, I was born looking like this.'

'God help your poor old ma if that was true.'

Her sisters ignored their host, striking a haughty pose of boredom and indifference, staring pointedly at the doors of the dance hall. Quickly Gallagher escorted them inside. The hall was rapidly filling with excited men and women. Gallagher hurried to the bandstand and yelled for attention.

'California Crossing welcomes old friends.'

A cheer broke out at this and he had a job calming the crowd enough to be heard.

'Today we are honoured to have as our guest the famous and most successful gold miner California has ever known.'

There were hoots of laughter from the floor and again Gallagher had to wait for calm before continuing.

'Mr O'Leary has paid for today's shenanigans. A big cheer for his generosity'

Again a bedlam of hooting, stamping of boots and cheers in the hall.

'There's plenty of food and drink – whiskey, beer and wine,' Gallagher went on when the noise subsided somewhat. 'Should be enough to satisfy the most pernickety amongst you. As my contribution, I've put barrels of water for you to dunk your heads in if you feel the need.' This last jest got him another chorus of guffaws and hoots. 'Just eat and drink and have a good time,' he yelled into the ensuing commotion.

Whatever else he wanted to say was superfluous, as the crowd lost no time in charging rowdily to the bar. At a signal from Gallagher, the fiddlers and harmonica players struck up a lively tune. Soon the hall was abuzz with music, talk, laughter and tobacco smoke.

When the celebrations were well under way, the old outlaw, in whose honour the party was being held, sauntered up to the band. The music ceased as he motioned to

them. Looking towards the bandstand, the mob of boisterous revellers saw what was happening and the noise fell
away. All heads turned expectantly towards the gang boss
waiting patiently for the crowd to quiet.

'Most of you are wondering what this celebration is all
about,' O'Leary began. 'Well, it's a goodbye party.'

There was some murmuring in the crowd but no one
interrupted.

'As you know I'm getting old – too old for the kinda life
I bin leading for the past . . . hell, I've lost count of the
years. Anyhow, it's time to hang up my spurs and let the
young 'uns take over.'

'No way, Keane. You're still top dog,' someone shouted.

'Yore a mite too young to hang up your spurs yet,
Keane.'

'There's life in the old dog yet.'

A murmur of similar sentiments rippled around the hall.
O'Leary held up his hands and the crowd quietened again.

'No, I've made my decision. I'm gonna put up my feet
and take it easy from now on.' He had to quieten the few
more shouts from the floor. 'However, I don't think the
bankers can breathe a sigh of relief just yet. Things will
carry on as before. Mostly 'cause I have children to carry on
the family tradition – my three lovely daughters, Gertrude,
Rachel and Catlin.'

Cheering broke out as O'Leary motioned his daughters
forward.

'I coulda done with having a son but the Good Lord
decided in his wisdom to bless me with three gals. I don't
know what the hell he was thinking but what the hell, a
man's gotta play the hand he's dealt in this life.

'Whatever, now that I'm stepping down I intend to split
my territory amongst my daughters. I have three fine
daughters and each will have a third of an area in which
there are rich pickings.' O'Leary smiled benignly at his

three offspring. 'What say you, Gertrude? How does this set with you?'

'Father, you are the best of men – a veritable lion. I'll be hard put to live up to your reputation.'

Gertrude had long black hair hanging to well below her shoulders. She favoured black leather clothing. Leather trews strained to contain her lower body. She wore a leather vest studded with silver. A tooled, black leather gun belt and Colt straddled generous hips. Her face was brooding with full sensual lips.

'To you, Gertrude, goes the southern part of our territory. And Rachel, my second daughter – to you goes the northern third. What do you say to that?'

Rachel stepped forward. In contrast to her sister she was flaxen-haired. She had the face of a cherub but there was a hardness to her eyes that she mostly hid from the world. She wore animal skins but favoured light coloured furs that matched her blonde locks. A cigarette dangled from her mouth as she spoke.

'No one could have had a better father than you. As my sister says, you are a lion among men. The name O'Leary will live on through your children.'

'Catlin.' The eyes softened as the old man looked at his youngest. 'For you the middle territory – the richest pickings of the whole region. What say you to that?'

Her broad handsome face was unsmiling as she stood before him. Like her sisters she too was armed, favouring a .44 thrust into the waistband of her denims.

'Nothing, Father. I want nothing.'

The old man looked slightly bemused.

'Nothing, come, come,' O'Leary said, a frown forming on his face. 'Is this some sort of joke?'

'Pa, I want to live my own life. I'm tired of living on the run. I want to live a normal life and not have to pack up and vamoose every time the law comes hunting us. Frank has asked me to go with him. We want to buy a horse ranch over in Nevada. All we ask is a stake. We'll need money to buy in stock.'

A silence fell across the hall. The only sounds the shuffling of boots on the boards.

'Catlin, of all my daughters you are most precious. Now think carefully. The middle region yields the most lucrative pickings. It's all yours along with the men to operate it. I have divided the territory in three. To you will go the best section. What say you to your old pa? Make an old man happy in the sunset of his life and reconsider.'

'Pa, I have considered long and hard. I want a life away from killing and thievery. Can't you understand that?'

The leathery face lost some of its colour. O'Leary's mouth twitched.

'Ungrateful child!' he hissed. 'Have I reared an unnatural brat in my household? You are an imp from the nether regions. For this insult to my legacy I disown you. From now on I have but two daughters. Get out of my sight! I never want to see you ever again.'

The blazing eyes suddenly focused on the tall, good-looking young man standing with his daughter.

'Frank!'

The name was spit out like a curse. A gun appeared in the old man's hand.

'No!' Catlin flung herself between her father and Frank. 'Pa, no!'

The Colt trembled in O'Leary's hand as his anger grew. Suddenly a shabby hirsute figure pushed forward to stand before O'Leary.

'For God's sake, Keane, this is your daughter! Put the gun up. This is no cause for gunplay.'

The fury of the bandit chief was transferred to the speaker.

'Cogan, get outta my way. This is my family and I'll settle

my own disputes.'

'No, Keane, I'll not stand by and let this happen. No way can this be settled by a shooting spree.'

'You intend to brace me, Cogan? You want to go out in the street and face me – man to man – gun against gun?'

'Keane, you know I'd go to hell and back for you. But this is madness. Your own daughter! Give her what she asks. You can afford to stake her and her man. They deserve better than this.'

'Nothing, nothing! I'll give them nothing!' The old man was almost spitting out the words. 'I have no daughter to give to. Get outta my sight. All of you! And you, Cogan – if you're here come sundown, I'm coming gunning for you.'

3

The pasteboards flicked out across the green baize. Monday Gallagher sat in his father's chair. The saloon was empty for it was late at night and the bar closed. Monday dealt poker hands and played against non-existent opponents. This was when he thought best – playing cards by himself, late at night. He was mulling over the happenings of the previous few days.

'My father calls me bastard and wishes I was other than half-breed. I think even a white bastard might have been more agreeable to him. But bastard! What did I do to deserve the name, bastard?'

He dealt two cards and contemplated his new hand.

'At O'Leary's jamboree, while I tended bar, my brother mixed with the guests. Am I not good enough to mix with my father's friends? I must be kept out of the way of decent folk. Huh! Decent folk! O'Leary and his gang are bandits and killers, but I'm not good enough even to mix with those one-percenters.'

Pushing back his chair, Monday drew a knife and thoughtfully tapped the blade against the edge of the table.

'If I cut myself, my blood is red just like my brother's. I have two things against me. My father lay with my mother but would not marry her. That makes me a bastard. My mother was a squaw. That makes me a half-caste. Two things

I have to overcome. In order to prosper, I must go away from here, which might bode an uncertain future.'

With a quick movement Monday flung the knife. It embedded in one of the wooden support columns.

'Or, I must rid myself of my family.'

Monday spread out the cards on the table.

'Flush beats a pair. My brother plays away from home tonight. I may make some gain from that.'

The youngster reached out and picked up the lantern from the table, retrieved the knife and slowly walked from the room.

Gallagher stood on the balcony overlooking the main street of California Crossing. He fiddled with a lighted cigar and stared out into the night sky. The town was quiet, for it was very late. Most of the drunks had gone home or were sleeping off their excesses in darkened alleys.

'Goddamn world's gone crazy. O'Leary gunning for Cogan. Catlin kicked outta the family. Is O'Leary mad?' The saloon owner shook his head in despair. 'It's a sad world when a father turns against his daughter. I'm glad I don't have daughters to make me mad. I have two fine sons to take care of me in my old age. But O'Leary. . . .'

The saloon owner leaned over to flick cigar ash into the street. As he did so a shot caromed from the alleyway, the muzzle flash lighting up the night's gloom. The bullet plucked at the shoulder of his jacket.

Gallagher's reactions were swift and he dropped to the floor and rolled back against the rear wall. He snatched his gun from the shoulder holster and lay there listening intently. He could hear nothing of any significance. Slowly he crawled to the corner of the balcony. Cautiously he raised his head and peered down towards the mouth of the alleyway from where the gunshot had come. He could see and hear nothing.

'Goddamn, dry-gulching son of a bitch,' he muttered and wriggled back towards the doorway.

Once inside he ran swiftly through and down the stairs. As he reached the bottom a figure appeared in the hallway.

'Stand fast or I'll shoot,' a voice challenged him.

'Monday, is that you?'

'Pa, what's going on? I heard a shot.'

'Someone's took a pot-shot at me from the alleyway. I'm going out back.'

'Jeez, Pa, let me get a light.'

'No time,' Gallagher flung back as he headed for the door.

The saloon owner poked his gun outside and peered from the doorway. In the faint moonlight he could distinguish nothing. Cautiously he stepped outside. He could hear the clatter of Monday somewhere inside as he hunted for a lantern.

Slowly he edged towards the corner of the building. Light suddenly spilled out behind him. Gallagher was about to call out a warning to the youngster when he thought better of it. The shooter would in all probability by now have made his escape.

'Pa.'

Monday moved up beside him, a lighted lantern in one hand and a revolver in the other.

'See anything?' he asked.

'Nah,' the older man replied. 'I guess he's long gone.'

Gallagher stared around the darkened alley. Monday moved into the opening, his lantern held high.

'For chris'sake, Monday, careful. The son of a bitch may still be out there.'

But his son was shuffling on into the alleyway. In spite of his misgivings Gallagher followed. They walked the full length of the alley, Monday holding the lantern aloft.

'No sign of anybody, Pa.'

They peered out into the main thoroughfare. Nothing moved in the silence of the sleeping town. The single shot had not disturbed anyone sufficiently to stir them to investigate.

'Who the hell would try to kill you, Pa?'

Monday turned and looked earnestly at his father.

'Beats me, son. I've made enough enemies in the past, though nothing recent comes to mind.'

Gallagher was shaking his head but still watching the shadows. He holstered his gun.

'Guess we might as well turn in. Ain't nothing to see out here.'

As they moved back down the side of the building, Monday gave a grunt and stopped.

'What is it?' Gallagher hissed, his nerves still taut.

'Just kicked agin' something.'

The lantern was lowered. A knife was lying on the ground, its blade shining in the light from the oil lamp. Gallagher grunted as he bent to retrieve it. Monday held the lamp close as they examined the knife.

'Son of a bitch!'

'What is it, Pa?'

Gallagher proffered the weapon to his son.

'You recognize this?' he asked.

Monday held the lantern higher and peered at the weapon.

'Sure,' he said. 'That's Alward's favourite knife. He never goes anywhere without that. He'll be real pleased we found it for him.'

There was silence as the older man turned the blade over and over in his hands.

'Does this suggest anything to you, Monday?'

'What do you mean, Pa? It's just Alward's knife is all.'

Gallagher was still turning the knife over and over in his hands.

'What's it doing in the alleyway?' he asked.

The lantern moved as the half-breed shrugged.

'He musta dropped it, is all. Mite careless of him.'

'You ever hear your brother say anything agin' me?'

'Nah, just the usual grumbles. Did brace me the other night after that O'Leary shindig. Wondered if you were thinking of retiring and letting him take over the running of things. But then he's always bitching on about that. I told him you had plenty of good years left in you yet.'

Gallagher could sense his son peering closely at him.

'You . . . you ain't thinking of retiring are you, Pa? I . . . I told him right, didn't I?'

'Yeah, son,' Gallagher said tightly. 'You told him right. Where is he now?' he asked as casually as he could.

'He said as he was going out riding,' Monday answered. 'Said as he wanted to sort things out in his mind. Don't think he's back yet.'

'Listen, son, don't say a word about this shooting. I'll hang on to the knife for now.' Gallagher tucked the knife into his pocket. 'And Monday, try and find out where Alward was tonight. Someone shot at me and I aim to find out who that son of a bitch was.'

Monday was turning to go when he stopped suddenly. Slowly he turned back, the lantern held high.

'Pa, you ain't thinking what I think you're thinking? No, no.' Monday was shaking his head. 'No way, Pa.'

Gallagher grabbed his son by the shirt front and pushed him up against the side of the building.

'Listen,' he hissed, 'someone took a shot at me tonight. I ain't ruling out nothing. Now if you know something about your brother, you spill it out now.'

'Jeez, Pa. I don't know what you're on about,' Monday whined. 'Alward and I, we ain't that close but . . . but. . . .'

Monday fell silent.

'But what?' Gallagher grated out. 'But what?'

'Nothing, Pa. Honest, I don't know nothing.'

Slowly Gallagher released his grip.

'Come on,' he growled. 'It's getting late. Let's get to bed. It'll be daylight afore we know it.'

The men disappeared inside the saloon, taking their lantern with them, leaving the alley in darkness.

4

The mule had a serene look about it that belied its nature. Cogan was not to know that. Having ridden horses most of his life, he knew nothing about mules. He had needed a mount and in his reduced circumstances, the mule was all he could afford. The stable hand that sold it to him lauded the animal's ability to go for days without food or water.

'That beast saved my life once. I was stranded out in the Sierras. Apaches had raided and taken everything. All I had 'tween me and survival was that there mule. She took me outta that wilderness. Wouldn't be here today to tell the story but for that there old gal.'

It hadn't occurred to Cogan to query why the ostler was willing to part with such a valuable beast at the knockdown price he was asking. He had paid the few dollars from his dwindling resources, purchased a dilapidated saddle and prepared to ride out.

The Cogan that negotiated the purchase of the mule was unrecognizable as the same man who had argued with O'Leary over his treatment of his youngest daughter. Gone were the masses of hair from face and head. A smooth-faced man now looked out at the world. Baggy overalls and plaid shirt had replaced the skins that had been his trademark ever since he had earned his living as a trapper.

Cogan's first inkling that he may have been hoodwinked

over the properties of the mule came when he went to saddle the beast. Casually the large grey head came around and two mean eyes regarded his efforts. Too quick for him to avoid entirely, large yellow teeth snapped shut on his hip.

'Goddamn bitch,' he swore, as he tried to prise loose from those deadly teeth.

Fortunately the overalls were a couple of sizes too big and the mule's jaws clamped on what was mostly a wad of fabric. Nevertheless the skin was nipped painfully. To make the mule loosen its grip, Cogan had to batter the animal on the nose with clenched fist. When finally released, he hopped about rubbing his hip and swearing long and luridly. The mule bared its teeth in a wicked grin.

'Goddamn bloody animal. I'd sell you for beef jerky only you'd probably poison anyone as chewed on it.'

The mule made a strange whickering sound and Cogan could have sworn the animal was laughing at him. He now approached the beast with extreme caution. So occupied was he watching for those snapping teeth he was unaware that as he tightened the girth, the mule was busily inflating its stomach. When he had the girth fastened, his next task was to get the bit in position.

Having considered the problem, Cogan edged round towards the rear of the animal. He had his knife in one hand and the bit in the other. Quickly he jammed the blade into the animal's rear end. The mule jumped, kicked out and at the same time opened its mouth to bray its displeasure. By this time Cogan was by the head and he jammed the bit in position – not without some risk to his fingers.

'Got you that time, you nasty little beastie,' he gloated, but his heart sank at the thought of having to go through all this every time he had to saddle up. If he hadn't been in such a hurry to vacate California Crossing, he might have considered confronting the man who had sold him this beast from hell.

From then on everything to do with the mule was performed while giving the wicked teeth and hoofs a wide berth. In spite of these precautions, the animal, at one stage, managed to stand on his foot.

'Hell's bells, if you ain't Satan's sister come to haunt me!' Cogan hollered, hopping about in agony for the second time. 'Hecate, that what I name you, Hecate. It was said of Hecate that even the wolves ran from her and the rats cowered in their holes when she came near.'

About two miles out of California Crossing, the newly christened Hecate allowed its stomach to deflate. She did this to the accompaniment of a loud sustained fart. Cogan was chuckling at this performance when the mule abruptly changed direction. The saddle tilted and Cogan, arms flailing as he tried to keep his balance, fell heavily on to the trail. Hecate continued blithely onwards as if unaware of the catastrophe that had befallen her new master.

'Goddamn it, maybe I should've faced down O'Leary,' the bruised man groaned. 'At least it would have been quick instead of this slow death by attrition.'

He picked himself up and hobbled painfully after the mule.

'Come back here, you harlot of Hades,' he yelled.

The mule let him almost catch it for a mile or more before she tired of the game and began to graze placidly on sage by the side of the road. Footsore and somewhat irked, Cogan warily approached the beast. He took out his revolver and placed the muzzle in the mule's ear.

'If you ever do that to me again I'm gonna blow your goddamn brains out of that evil skull of yours.'

The mule regarded him calmly out of one jaundiced eye then pursed its lips and snickered. Cogan knew the mule was calling his bluff. The animal had set the limits of her new master's dominance. Cogan realized he was in a no-win situation. Wearily he set about the arduous task of tightening up the saddle girth and remounting.

'Hecate, only one of us will walk away from this here relationship and I ain't sure I'm gonna be the one left standin'.'

5

One of the hideouts used by the O'Leary gang was a horse ranch called Barren Drum, set way back in the hills. It may have been this ranch that gave Catlin and Frank the idea of setting up their ranch. It was a sprawling mess of buildings with extensive corrals used to contain the horses brought in for breaking. As well as being a hideaway, the ranch also furnished the outlaws with replacement mounts.

It was here O'Leary had decided to retire after leaving California Crossing. He, and the few gunmen he retained as bodyguards, idled their time away either playing cards or hunting. It was late in the day after one of these expeditions that the gang rode into the yard. One of the riders hefted a small deer that had been lashed behind his saddle.

'Ain't much to show for a day's hunting, Keane,' the man commented.

'Huh, I been out holding up a wagon train and got less than that for all my efforts. At least we can have that deer for dinner some evening.'

The men were boisterous as they spilled into the ranch house. The main room was set out as a dining area with rough benches and tables.

'Take that down to the cook and tell him we'll have it tomorrow or the day after,' O'Leary instructed the man with the deer. 'And tell him to hurry up with dinner.'

There was a crash as a fight broke out and one of the benches overturned. O'Leary banged on a table with his riding crop and called for order. But his men were crowding around the fighters and urging them on. No one heard the outlaw chief and in the end, he gave up his efforts and joined the onlookers. Someone tugged at his sleeve.

'Fella here to see you here, boss.'

O'Leary turned impatiently and Marcus Cogan was standing before him grinning broadly.

'Yeah, what the hell are you grinning at like a loon with no brain?' O'Leary asked, not recognizing his former scout and friend, now shorn of his long hair and beard and minus his animal skins.

Cogan took a battered black hat from his head.

'I need a job, boss.'

'A job,' hooted O'Leary, 'what can you do?'

'I can ride a she-devil of a mule, shoot a gun, bend a nail in my teeth, drink a gallon of whiskey at one sitting and keep a whore happy for half a night.'

O'Leary laughed heartily at such blatant bluster.

'OK, fella. If you can stop that fight I'll give you a start.'

By now they had to shout to be heard above the noise of riotous men. Cogan handed his hat to a bemused O'Leary.

'I just rode thirty miles on the mule from hell. Compared to that, stopping these fellas will be easy.'

Without more ado the newcomer waded into the crowd. Men were unceremoniously shunted aside until at last Cogan reached the fighters. He took out his gun and waiting for the right opportunity, cracked one of the fighters on the back of the head with it.

The man staggered but did not go down. He turned indignantly to face his new attacker. That was a mistake. His opponent clubbed him and he sagged at the knees and collapsed on the floor. Cogan nodded to the second fighter who grinned back at him. O'Leary was laughing as Cogan returned to him. He handed the new man his hat.

'You'll do, fella, you're hired. What's your name?'

Cogan grinned and bowed. 'I'm called Hillard, boss.'

'Well, I'll call you Hard Hill for short,' O'Leary told him. 'How does that fit?'

'The last time I got a new name the sky-pilot tried to drown me in a rain butt. As long as you don't try to do the same that'll do me.'

O'Leary laughed again. 'You'll do, fella.' He banged on the table with his crop. 'Dinner, where the hell's that dinner? I'm so hungry I could eat a skunk's backside.'

By this time the man who had taken the deer to the kitchens had returned.

'Son of a bitch ain't even started dinner yet,' he complained to the bandit chief.

In the midst of the clamour a big overblown man came into the room. O'Leary recognized him as one of his former riders now serving his daughter.

'Lovell,' he called, 'where's Gertrude? And what's going on? My man tells me the cook hasn't even started cooking dinner yet.'

The big man eyed O'Leary coolly before replying.

'You'll have to get your own meals from now on. Lady Gertrude says cook has rebelled and refuses to cater for so many.'

'Rebelled!' O'Leary roared. 'Send the son of a bitch up to me. I'll soon put the rebellion out of him.' O'Leary slapped the table with his riding crop. 'A good whipping will soon knock the starch outta him. On second thoughts, staking him out on an anthill would be a more fittin' punishment. Get him up here at once.' He paused a moment. 'What's all this lady business? Since when have you been calling Gertrude lady?'

'I'm sorry, Mr O'Leary, but I answer only to my mistress.'

O'Leary's eyes narrowed. 'You what, you cur? You'll

answer me when I say so.'

Lovell backed away, his hand on his gun. Before O'Leary could respond to this act of insubordination, someone pushed past him. His new hand flung himself at Lovell, taking the man by surprise. Cogan's gun slashed across the man's face. Lovell cried out and stumbled back, tugging at his pistol. Cogan was merciless. Again and again he beat the man across his head. Blood splashed onto his shirt and Lovell fell to the floor, cowering before his attacker.

O'Leary's men were crowding around the pair and cheering. Suddenly there was a commotion in the doorway. Men with drawn guns were spilling into the room.

'Enough!'

The shrill voice of O'Leary's daughter cut into the noise like a whiplash.

'Enough!'

Gertrude pushed forward and looked from Cogan to the bleeding man on the floor. Her eyes, cold and hard, focussed on Cogan. She looked at the gun in the newcomer's hand.

'Put up that weapon.'

'Gertrude, Gertrude.' O'Leary confronted his daughter. 'What's the meaning of this?' He swept his hand round at the group of armed men. 'Coming in here with guns! I'm your father, for God's sake.'

The cold eyes were turned on the old man.

'Father, when you gave up your leadership you agreed to spend some time with me and time with Rachel. But we did not agree to have a mob of hellions rampaging through the place. I'll not have your oafs fighting with my men. Look at the state of this place. It's like a madhouse. I'm in command here. You obey my rules or face the consequences.'

'Gertrude, what are you saying?'

O'Leary had gone pale. His daughter looked at him, her

face hard and unyielding.

'If your men want to behave like animals then they can live like animals. From now on this trash can stay out in the stables. They will not be allowed inside the house again.'

'And what about me, Gertrude?' The old man's voice trembled with anger. 'Am I to be banished to the stables also?'

'You, my dear father, may come and go as you please. But you will not order my men to do anything for you, nor will you abuse them as you have poor Lovell here.'

'Your men . . . your men. . . !' The words were spluttered out as the old man tried to rein in his growing anger. 'You have these men 'cause I chose to give them to you. Up until that they owed their allegiance to me.'

O'Leary stared round at the ring of Gertrude's gunmen. Some looked away as if embarrassed by the plight of their old chief but most stared him out.

'And what about Alec?' O'Leary asked. 'How does he figure in this?'

It was then he noticed the blond gunman lounging in the doorway.

'Alec, what way is this to treat me? I hope you haven't got a hand in this.'

Alec took the cigarette from his mouth and casually tapped at the ash. He looked coolly back at the old man.

'It's Gertrude's call, Keane. She's top bitch now. I'm only married to her.' He shrugged. 'I'll just have to back her play.'

'A fiend. I have raised a fiend in my house—' O'Leary spluttered before being interrupted by his daughter.

'You men, out!' she yelled. 'From now on you fend for yourselves. I don't care how, but my hospitality ceases as of now. Get them out, boys.'

O'Leary stood helplessly as his men were herded out the doorway. They kept looking to him for guidance but the old man seemed dazed by the unrelenting swiftness of his daughter's actions. Suddenly he snapped out of his bewilderment.

'Saddle up, men,' he shouted. 'I'll abide no more in this house. I have banished one daughter and cherished a viper. Saddle up.' He turned and glared venomously at Gertrude. 'I will go to Rachel. I will find charity with Rachel. I curse you, vixen that you are. I curse the day a she-devil entered into my home. You are a vixen that somehow crept into my household.'

The scorn in his daughter's eyes finally drove the old man after his men. Cogan warily watched his back as they left the room. As the routed men made preparations for their journey, O'Leary called Cogan to his side.

'I want you to go on ahead and take this note to my daughter Rachel. Tell her we are for California Crossing and then on to her place to stay with her. Oh, the ingratitude of children. I tell you this, Hard Hill, don't have children. They'll cast you out in your old age.'

Rachel's share of the O'Leary inheritance was a way station called Pearly Gates. It was another of the bandit king's hideouts. Though he knew quite well the whereabouts of the way station, Cogan feigned ignorance of its location.

'Ride to California Crossing,' O'Leary told him. 'It's on the way to Pearly Gates. Ask for Gallagher. He'll give you directions.'

6

Alward Gallagher acknowledged that Xaviera was exceedingly beautiful, but the shack she called home was decidedly slovenly. He rubbed a hand over his face and felt the three-day stubble.

Not much chance of a shave in this pigpen, he thought ruefully. He would have to wait until he got back home. Still, it had been a wonderful couple of days' indulgence with the young Mexican dancer.

Idly he wondered how his father and Monday were coping without him. Alward sighed and decided he would have to make the effort and return home. The girl buried under the skins covering the bed stirred.

'*Señor* Alward,' she murmured sleepily.

Her hand came across and stroked his bare chest and he became instantly aroused.

'Xaviera, your name is as exotic as your lovely self.'

He rolled on top of her. Her hand came up and stroked his bristles.

'My skin, is she rub raw. But I not mind my preetty boy, Alward. You good loveer. We make pleenty good happy together.'

The black eyes that smiled up at him were sunk beneath slender eyebrows. Tousled jet-black hair made a perfect

frame for clear olive skin. Her blood-red lips were inviting
him to sink his tongue into the juicy rich plumpness.
Hardened nipples pressed against his chest as he lowered
himself on top of her.

'Mmmm . . .' she moaned, 'my beautiful Alward.'

Afterwards, in the warm glow of intimacy, the youngster
lay back in the bed, suffused with love for his lovely companion.

'I make the breakfast for my beeautiful man.'

She kissed him on the nose and looked longingly into his
eyes.

'You the best loveer for Xaviera,' the young woman murmured. 'I love you always, my beautiful Alward.'

'Don't worry none about breakfast, Xaviera,' Alward told
her. 'It's OK. I really gotta go.'

'No. My man weel not go hungry. I not allow you leeve
here with empty belly.'

He lay lazily in the bed and watched the voluptuous
Xaviera as she busied herself preparing corn tortillas for his
breakfast.

'I weel feed my man and make heem strong. You weel
need plenty strong to look after your Xaviera.'

Alward grinned. If the last three days were anything to
go by, he certainly would need stamina.

While Alward Gallagher whiled away his days in lovemak-
ing, Monday Gallagher was rummaging around in his
brother's living quarters. He was humming gently as he
searched.

Now the coyote hunted wide that night.
An' as he hunted he prayed for light.
With many a mile to go that night,
Before he caught a bobwhite,
Bobwhite, bobwhite.

He'd many a mile to go that night,
Before he caught a bobwhite.

'Ah!'

Monday held up a blue, silk shirt. Neatly embroidered on each pocket in shining red thread were his brother's initials. Rolling the distinctive shirt in a bundle, he stuffed it inside his jacket and left the room, still humming the hunting song.

When Alward rode into California Crossing, he was unaware his half-brother watched for his return. Once Monday had spotted him and knew his brother was returning home, he saddled his own horse and rode out of town. Monday had told his father he did not know where his brother had been. However, Monday knew exactly where his sibling was.

Monday kept track of Alward's comings and goings and was well aware that his brother spent his time in the Mexican village with a young woman. Now he retraced Alward's route back to the shack of his Mexican lover.

Outside the village, Monday hid his horse in a group of trees. He took the silk shirt he had purloined from Alward's room from his saddle bag and changed it for his own. Attired in the silk shirt, he made his way cautiously towards the girl's shack and after making sure no one was about, he stepped inside. At first he thought the place was empty. Then the bed covers heaved.

'My beeautiful Alward, you have return.'

Xaviera's tousled hair emerged and she stared sleepily at the man standing by the bed.

'Alward?' Suddenly her eyes widened. 'Monday! Is Alward . . . he is OK?'

'Yes, your beautiful Alward is fine – for now anyway. He asked me to come and sample your delights. Said as you were great fun in the bedroom.'

The blue silk shirt almost glowed in the dimness of the shack as she glared at him.

'Alward, he would not do that,' the girl said, in a low distressed voice.

As the man made an effort to get in bed with her, she clutched the covers to her.

'Get out!' she hissed, anger beginning to take over from her bewilderment. 'Get out!'

Monday punched her full in the face. She gave a small cry and let go her grip on the bedclothes. Her hands were on her face and blood leaked from her nose, staining the fingers. She opened her mouth to scream as Monday rolled onto the bed. He grabbed up a crumpled bed sheet and jammed it into her mouth

Her eyes opened wide. She clenched her bloodied hands and pounded them against his chest. Monday raised himself up and punched her viciously in the stomach. Her muffled screams grew weaker and weaker. But all the time she fought him – her nails tearing at the silk shirt and smearing it with blood.

'You know, Alward was right,' Monday panted as he fastened his hands round the girl's neck. 'You are a real fiery woman. I could love you to death.'

Her eyes began to bulge as he squeezed. The hands that had been ripping at the silk shirt, leaving tiny rips and smears of blood, now clawed at the fingers clamped round her throat.

Alward came in the saloon and nodded a greeting to his father. Gallagher glared balefully at his son.

'Where the hell've you been?' Gallagher growled.

Before answering, the youngster walked behind the bar and poured himself a whiskey. He was still glowing from the effects of his love tryst with the lithe Mexican dancer.

'Hi, Pa, I rode out a ways. Didn't go nowhere in particular.'

The youngster was wary of his father learning of his relationship with Xaviera. Ever since Gallagher's dalliance with Monday's mother, he frowned on mixing the races.

'I sent Monday out looking for you,' Gallagher told him. 'Thought you might be in trouble.'

The saloon owner moved to the bar and stood leaning against it, watching his son closely.

'Trouble, nah, no trouble,' Alward assured him.

'I ain't seen much of you since O'Leary's shindig,' Gallagher pressed on. 'Wondered where you got to.'

'Pa, I'm nearly eighteen years of age now. I'm old enough to take care of myself. I don't need to answer to you twenty-four hours a day. And I don't need no wet-nurse brother looking after my interests.'

The two men stood eyeing each other.

'You a growed man now. Maybe think you should be running your own show.'

'Well, Pa, now that you mention it I could do with a bit more independence. What if I wanted to marry and set up house? Can't bring a wife back here now, can I? It's an all bachelor establishment.'

'You want to set up on your own? Maybe with me out of the way it would be a durn sight easier for you.'

'What the hell sort of talk's that? I ain't talking about you. I'm talking about me. I got a life to live or did you think I ought to stay around here and look after you in your old age while I grow old myself?'

'Mebby you'd like me to retire just like O'Leary,' the older man gritted out. 'Then you could mebby take over.'

'Pa, what the hell are you talking about? You know you love this business. You won't retire. The only way you'll leave here is in a wooden box.'

Gallagher's head snapped up.

'You son of a bitch. It was you. Monday tried to dissuade me different.'

To the youngster's astonishment a gun was suddenly pushed against his chest and when he looked into his father's eyes, he saw cold fury in them. Alward stood very still.

'Pa,' he whispered, 'have you gone mad? It's me, Alward. Alward Gallagher – your son. What the hell's going on, pulling a gun?'

For answer the older man produced a knife and slid it on the bar.

'Recognize this?'

Alward examined the knife without picking it up.

' 'Course I recognize it. It's my knife. Monday bought it me one birthday. What you doing with it?'

'Someone took a shot at me last night. This knife was found where the son 'a bitch fired. Now I ask you again. Where were you last night?'

'Pa . . . you ain't suggesting . . . Jeez, Pa . . .' Alward's voice faded as he stared into the unrelenting eyes of his father. 'This is madness.'

'You ain't gonna tell me, are you?'

In desperation, and thinking his father had indeed gone mad, Alward weakened and told his father where he had spent the last few days.

'That Mexican slut, is that the best you can come up with?'

'For goddamn's sake, ask her! She and I were in her shack all the time. You can ask her. She'll tell you I ain't stirred from there until now.'

'Mexes are well known liars. No doubt she'll lie for you – her big boy lover.'

Whatever reply Alward was about to make was never said. At that moment the saloon doors banged open and people spilled inside. Rachel and Cornwell stood smirking across at the Gallaghers while more and more of their gunhands drifted through the swing doors.

'Gallagher, we've come to sample your hospitality and do a mite of business.'

'Rachel, what a pleasant surprise,' Gallagher enthused. 'Come on in. Let me get you drinks.' Gallagher turned to Alward. 'Set 'em up, boy.' And added in a lower tone, 'Don't you disappear again. You and I have unfinished business.'

7

'Take a fast horse and ride to my sister and deliver this letter to her.' Gertrude held a sealed envelope in her hand as she spoke. 'Rachel has sent me word she and Cornwell are going to California Crossing on some business with Gallagher. Tell her what has happened here. Keep this letter secure. Make sure only she gets it. Alec and I will follow at our leisure. We should all meet at Gallagher's place. Only make sure you get to Rachel before O'Leary.'

Lovell saluted his mistress and made preparations to leave. He was aware of the uproar amongst O'Leary's followers as they packed their belongings and made ready to leave on the trip to Pearly Gates. Seeing the confusion amongst the men, Lovell calculated he had plenty of time to call on the brothel in California Crossing before delivering Gertrude's letter to her sister.

He galloped out from the ranch; his urgency prompted more by the necessity of slaking his lust than any loyalty to his mistress. There were few travellers on the trail. Lovell took little or no notice of the ones he did encounter. The rider cantering towards California Crossing on a large mule did not even warrant a glance.

It was fortunate that O'Leary did not witness his chosen messenger readying his mount for departure or he may have had some misgivings. Not wanting to risk his 'mount-from-hell' fighting with other animals at the ranch, Cogan had housed the mule in a disused barn. And so he was able to get ready for his mission without anyone observing his difficulties. By using a mixture of threats, blows and cunning, he and his ill-tempered mule eventually got underway.

It was late when Cogan arrived at California Crossing. He made his way to the livery and off-saddled. By now he had become quite accomplished at avoiding snapping teeth and stomping hoofs. There was no one on duty at the livery stable and most of the stalls were in use so he tethered Hecate well to the back of the building.

'Hecate, I don't know whether to shoot you or just abandon you here.'

He was emerging from the building when a rider pulled up.

'You there, take care of this horse,' the man ordered, obviously mistaking Cogan for the liveryman.

'Take care of it yourself, you fat oaf. Or maybe you're so dumb you don't know how.'

'Fella, you better have more respect for me. I work for the O'Leary sisters.'

Gertrude's messenger was clearly drunk, having managed to down a fair amount of liquor while indulging himself at the whorehouse.

'Now do as you're told. I'm late as it is.'

'Huh! Work for the O'Learys, do you!' Cogan said, well aware of the identity of the traveller. 'What do you do? Clean out the cesspit for them?'

'You son of a bitch. I'm gonna whip your ass.'

'You'll wipe my ass you mean, or if you're referring to my misbegotten mule, she's tethered down there. I'm betting she'll come out the winner in any fight with a butt ugly son of a bitch like you.'

As Lovell went to dismount, Cogan reached out and

gripped his boot.

'Let me help you down,' he offered.

A quick heave and Lovell tumbled out of the saddle, landing heavily on the dirt.

'Goddamn your hide!'

Lovell was lumbering to his feet when Cogan kicked him savagely on the shoulder. The big man tumbled out into the street.

'You wanted to wipe my ass, so stay on your knees,' Cogan called gleefully.

Lovell tried to rise and this time, Cogan's kick caught him in the rear end. In his efforts to escape his attacker, Lovell stumbled away from the stables.

Again and again Cogan kicked the man, driving him further and further along the street. Cogan gave the big man no time to go for a weapon even if he had been so inclined. Each time Lovell tried to rise, Cogan kicked him.

The pair progressed along the street with Lovell cursing and yelling at his attacker and Cogan calling him whatever offensive names he could dredge up. The hubbub brought people into street. Gallagher, along with Rachel and Cornwell, came out to see the fun.

'Hold on there,' Gallagher called, not recognizing Cogan in his new guise. 'Why are you attacking this fella?'

Cogan paused, his chest heaving from the effort of kicking his enemy all the way from the livery.

'This dog threatened to kick my ass. I'm giving him lessons on how it's done.'

Lovell looked up hopefully at the crowd and as he did so, he noticed Rachel.

'I have a message from Gertrude,' he called in desperation. 'I was on my way to deliver it when this animal attacked me and tried to rob me.'

Cogan's boot on the side of Lovell's head stopped anything else he might have said.

'He's a liar as well as a coward,' raged Cogan, aiming another kick.

'Stop! For God's sake, stop!'

Rachel's husband, Cornwell, stepped forward and pushed Cogan back from the cowering man. Cornwell was a handsome man with jet-black hair and a dark bushy moustache. He was tall with the broad shoulders of an athlete. He stared down at Lovell.

'You say you come from Gertrude?' Cornwell asked.

'I have a letter from her. She sent me to deliver it to Rachel.'

'Get up,' Cornwell commanded and turned to Cogan. 'You're in trouble, fella. You picked the wrong man to rob. No one messes with the O'Learys.'

'If I wanted to rob that coward I'd have killed him first instead of beating him. I've come from O'Leary himself. And this letter is for Miss Rachel.'

Cogan produced the missive and made to hand it to Rachel. Cornwell reached out for it.

'It's for Miss Rachel,' Cogan protested. 'It's from her father.'

At that moment Lovell raised his hand and pointed.

'I recognize him now. That's the bastard as attacked me at Barren Drum and insulted Gertrude.'

Rachel stepped forward and snatched the note from Cogan's unresisting fingers.

'Insult my sister!' she snarled. 'What sort of company is O'Leary keeping now?'

She stepped back into the lamplight. Quickly she scanned both notes.

'As God is my witness I never insulted your sister,' Cogan protested. 'Like I said afore, this fella's a liar as well as a coward.'

Rachel nodded curtly to her men.

'Take him,' she ordered.

'What the. . . ?'

Cogan stood no chance as Rachel's henchmen quickly grabbed him.

'You there,' the blonde woman called to Lovell, 'now's your chance to get even.'

Lovell walked over to Cogan, now firmly pinioned by two of Rachel's gunnies. The big man had a smirk on his chubby face as he approached. He backhanded Cogan who immediately kicked him. Hollering, Lovell hopped back out of range.

'Get him on his knees,' Rachel shrieked at the gunnies.

Without more urging they clubbed and kicked their captive to make him kneel in the dirt. Seeing his tormentor helpless, Lovell ventured forward once more and booted Cogan in the midriff. The stricken man grunted and hung over, gasping for breath. Then the burly man really set to work on the helpless Cogan.

Lovell rained down vicious punches and kicks. As the beating progressed, no one was sure if the victim was conscious or not. Each time Lovell landed a blow, blood sprayed from cuts on the ruptured face and nose. In the end it was Gallagher who stepped in to end the brutal beating.

'That's enough. If what he says is true and O'Leary sent him it ain't gonna set too well if he finds his messenger dead.'

'Take him down the livery and leave him there,' Cornwell ordered.

The bloodied man was dragged back down the street to the livery and slung inside with Lovell trailing behind, piling curses on the unresponsive Cogan.

'Next time our paths cross I'll kill you,' Lovell snarled, as he planted a parting kick on the semi-conscious Cogan.

Painfully Cogan dragged himself further inside the stables. Like any wounded animal, he wanted to curl up in a dark corner. At last he rested against a back wall, slipping in and out of a black void.

He wasn't sure, but it seemed that through the mists of pain, something soft and moist was caressing his face. Barely able to open pain-dazed eyes, he peered up at his benefactor. For a horrible moment he saw the face of his mule and then he passed into oblivion.

8

His face covered with lather, Alward Gallagher stropped his razor. He had a thick head of ginger hair which he kept cropped short. His regular features and deep green eyes gave him a look of gravity. Before applying the soap to his beard, he had stood before the mirror and admired the light stubble on his face, thinking it made him look more mature. Absently stropping the blade of the cutthroat along the leather, he mulled over the conversation with his father. Fine lean muscles rippled across his youthful torso as he worked.

The disturbance out front in the street engaged his attention and he crossed to the window and watched with interest the little drama between the protagonists. His sympathies were with the man being beaten by the fat man. For a moment he toyed with the idea of intervening, but his own problems were foremost in his mind regarding the strange behaviour of his father. Eventually the action ceased as the stricken man was dragged away. The onlookers went back in the saloon and Alward returned to his ablutions.

'Goddamn it, what's the matter with Pa?' he muttered into the shaving glass. 'It's like he were a different man. All I did was go sparking Xaviera. Jeez, didn't he hook up with a damn squaw? Maybe that's it. He don't want no more half-breed kids in the family.'

Alward shook his head in bewilderment and lifted the razor to his face. Before he could begin his shave, another commotion in the street stopped him.

'What the hell's going on now?'

With the razor held in his hand he went to the window and peered outside. There was a lot of shouting and he could see a bunch of Mexicans milling around on the street. Frowning, he opened the window the better to hear what the men were shouting about. Behind him the door burst open. Alward whirled, his nerves tense. Monday stood in the doorway panting heavily.

'Oh, it's you,' Alward growled. 'What the hell's that racket all about? What's up with those Mexicans?'

'Al, Al you gotta run! Them Mexes are after your blood. They're saying you killed Xaviera.'

'Xaviera! What the hell are you on about? I just left her earlier today. What's going on?'

'Come on. Get out the back while I hold them off. I told them it was all nonsense but they're mighty riled up and want your blood. They found your shirt in Xaviera's cabin. They're liable to string you up.'

As Monday was talking he was manhandling his brother towards the door.

'Goddamn it, Monday, will you stop hassling me? I ain't done nothing. And what are you saying about Xaviera?'

'Al, listen to me. I'm your brother and I believe you and I'd do anything to protect you. Let me handle this. You light out and hide in the hills. I'll calm them down and come for you when the heat is off.'

'But . . . Monday . . . I . . . .'

'Al, please!' Monday spoke earnestly. 'They're in a dangerous mood. Someone killed your Mexican lover and they're blaming you. They're so riled up anything might

happen. Let me calm them down and get them to listen.
But right now you gotta get well away from here.'

Loud voices suddenly broke out below. Shots were fired
accompanied by the sounds of breaking glass.

'For God's sake, Al, they're in no mood to listen. They'll
string you up afore you have a chance to prove your inno-
cence. Your only chance is to make a run for it. Go out to
that old shack at Mule Back Mine. No one will ever think of
looking for you there. I'll come and fetch you when it's safe
and these damn Mexes are sent packing.'

The angry voices were becoming louder though no more
shots sounded.

'Take my horse,' Monday urged. 'It's out back, saddled
and ready. Now, go, go. For God's sake, go.'

Such was the urgency and force of Monday's urging,
Alward allowed himself to be pushed out of the back door.
He was shirtless and his face was covered in shaving soap. In
his hand he still clutched his razor. Before he could gather
his wits, he was on Monday's horse and threading his way
along back alleys and out into the night. It never occurred
to him to wonder why Monday's horse was tied up so con-
veniently at the rear door of the saloon, saddled and ready
to go. Monday watched his brother ride out of sight.

'Ride, Alward, ride,' he whispered. 'Ride out of my life.'

Monday pulled his knife and with a quick movement,
slashed his arm with the blade and knelt in the dirt.

'Help, help! Stop, stop! Someone stop him!'

Shortly his father burst out of the door. More and more
men piled into the alley. To Monday's gratification he saw
they were the Mexicans.

'Pa. It were Al. I tried to stop him. He cut me and run.
Jeez, my arm hurts.'

'Which way he go?' demanded one of the Mexicans.

'I . . . I don't know. He . . . he just slashed me an' . . . I
was trying to get away from him and then he grabbed a

horse and went. I . . . I didn't notice where he was headed.'

More and more bodies were spilling out of the back of the saloon. The hubbub of voices grew as the new arrivals tried to find out what was happening. Monday felt a soft touch on his arm. He turned to find Rachel beside him.

'You poor boy, you're bleeding. Let me tend to that.'

Monday followed the blonde gang leader inside. Behind them the Mexicans were rushing back through the saloon, vowing to find the murderer.

'We'll go to your room,' Rachel said. 'I'll be better able to attend you away from this here racket.'

Once inside his room Rachel tended the cut. It was not deep and she was able to stem the bleeding and bind it with a towel. As she worked Monday noticed her blouse was undone. Through the opening he could see the soft swell of her breasts. She looked into his eyes and smiling gently, lifted his good hand and pushed it inside her blouse.

'You're a very fine looking young man, Monday,' she murmured softly.

Monday was becoming aroused – his hand buried inside Rachel's clothing. But still he was cautious.

'What about Cornwell?'

Her capable hands were working on his belt and then his trousers were being manoeuvred down over his hips.

'Cornwell?' Her eyebrows arched gracefully. 'He's probably on his second bottle of rye by now.'

She pulled his head down and their lips met.

9

It was well past midday when O'Leary led his men into California Crossing. The settlement was comparatively quiet after the excitement of the previous evening. As the riders pulled up outside the livery a rumble of thunder could be heard in the distance.

'Glad we got shelter for the night,' one rider commented. 'I don't like the look of that there sky.'

O'Leary grunted. He was still churning over the events that had driven him from Barren Drum. An old man with a grizzled beard and toothless gums appeared in the doorway.

'Full house, gents. Never knowed so many visitors to the town. All I have is the corral out back. If you care, I'll feed and water your mounts. Cost two bits a horse.'

He waited expectantly while the men dismounted.

'Dangest thing,' the old-timer remarked. 'Got a fella in there bin beat up some. There's this big mule watching over him. Won't let me near the poor man.'

Only half listening, O'Leary looked up at the mention of a mule.

'A mule you say. Joe, have a look. That new hand I sent on to Rachel rode a mule. Oh hell, might as well go myself.'

The inside of the barn was dim. At one end a large mule turned a baleful eye towards the men crowding through the doorway. A figure could be seen climbing painfully to his feet. He clung to the boards of the stalls and then hooking an arm around the mule's neck, he shuffled forward.

'Hard Hill? Is that you, Hard Hill?'

Man and mule moved slowly forward into the light. Cogan's features were swollen to grotesque proportions. Though his face was clear of gore, dark bruises and cuts disfigured his skin. His shirt was caked with dried blood.

'Damnation, Hard Hill, you bin sparring with that there doggone mule?'

'Boss, I thought I heard your voice. Sorry about all this. Got myself in a mite of trouble.'

'Who did this to you? Who did this?'

'Your daughter's man, Lovell – with some help from Rachel's men.'

'Rachel! Is she here? And her men beat you up! You're crazy, man. I sent you with a message for Rachel. She wouldn't dare abuse you.'

'She did so. That son of a bitch, Lovell, came with a message from Gertrude. I was kicking his ass when Rachel and Cornwell rescued him and then did this to me.'

'Hard Hill, I'll pistol-whip you if you persist. Rachel would not treat one of my men so.'

Cogan shrugged and then winced as his bruised body protested at the sudden movement.

'Why don't you ask her, boss? She's up at Gallagher's place.'

O'Leary swung around.

'You men tend the horses,' he ordered. 'Then follow me over to Gallagher's.'

The gang boss stalked from the barn.

'You gonna be all right, Hill?' Joe enquired.

'I feel like I've gone ten rounds with a she-bear. Though I don't think anything's broke.'

'Looks like someone cleaned you up pretty good –

washed the blood off.'

'Damnedest thing.'

Cogan turned and stared at the big grey beast standing docilely behind him.

'I bin fighting this here mule for days now. It tried to bite and stomp me and then when I crawled in here to curl up and die, it must've licked my face clean and watched over me all night.' Cogan shook his head. 'Damnedest thing.'

Cornwell, Gallagher, Monday and Rachel were gathered at a table in earnest conversation when O'Leary entered the saloon. Only Gallagher, used to scrutinizing everyone that crossed his threshold, noticed him come in. The saloon owner jumped up, a welcoming smile on his face.

'By Jupiter, if it ain't like old times again,' he enthused. 'My good friend Keane O'Leary.'

Rachel raised a beckoning hand.

'Pa, oh, Pa, it's good to see you,' she called.

Neither Cornwell nor Monday acknowledged the old man.

'Rachel, it's good to see you, too. But what are you doing here? I was on my way to Pearly Gates.'

'What? What for? Weren't you were staying with Gertrude?'

'Rachel, my dear girl, you'll hardly believe what I have to tell you. Your sister, Gertrude, she . . . she threw me out of Barren Drum. Can you believe it?'

'Father, Father, you must have done something really bad to annoy her. She wouldn't behave like that without good reason.'

'What! What reason could she have for treating her own father like a . . . a. . . .'

Words failed him and he stared at his daughter with distraught face.

'But I'll come to you,' he finally managed. 'You won't treat your old pa so.'

'Come to me! Well, I . . . I wasn't ready for you yet. You were to stay with Gertrude for a mite longer. I wasn't expecting you so soon.'

O'Leary stared with a distraught face at his daughter.

'Rachel, what are you saying – you're not ready for me? I'm your father. We made a bargain. You got half of what I had. I was to spend my time between Gertrude and you.'

'Yes, yes, dear Father, but you can see I am not at Pearly Gates to receive you right now. Just be a good man and return to Barren Drum. I'll expect you later in the year. I'll be ready for you then.'

For a moment O'Leary's eyes took on a baffled look and then his face began to twitch. He opened his mouth a couple of times as if to speak but no sound came. Standing beside them, Gallagher stared from daughter to father. He intervened in what was an effort to rescue the old man from further embarrassment.

'Let me get you a drink, Keane. What'll it be – whiskey?' Then remembering in time O'Leary's latest taste for wine. 'Got a new cask of wine come in the last shipment. Thought mebby you'd like to sample it.'

The saloon owner might have been talking to a deaf mute for all the notice O'Leary took of him.

'Who beat my man?' O'Leary ground out through clenched teeth. 'I sent my man to you to inform you of my arrival. I just found him half beat to death out in the livery stable. Who did that?'

'I did.'

The answer came not from Rachel but from her half-drunken husband. Rachel glanced at the surly face of Cornwell but said nothing.

'You insolent bastard, Cornwell, I'll . . . I'll thrash your hide . . . you. . . .'

There was the scraping of chair legs on the wooden floor. Cornwell stood upright, swaying slightly. His hand rested on the butt of his holstered gun.

'What you gonna do, old man?'

The gunman emphasized the last two words with a hint of contempt in his tone. O'Leary's mouth was working but no sound came. He stepped back a pace or two and at that moment his own men came in the door. Oblivious of the tension in the room they crowded around their leader.

'What about a drink, boss?'

'My tongue's like a piece of dried out saddle leather.'

'Sure is thirsty work, all this riding.'

'Sure, sure,' Gallagher said, and took O'Leary by the arm. 'Drinks on the house. Come on, Monday. Let's get these boys a drink. They've come a long way to slake their thirst .'

Unresisting, O'Leary was hustled to the bar surrounded by his jabbering men. The old man placed his hands on the bar and Gallagher noticed the tremor in them. As he served up the drinks, the saloon owner talked animatedly in an effort to distract his old friend.

Monday came over behind the bar to assist. Cornwell was sitting again but he was glowering across at O'Leary's men. Gallagher was congratulating himself on defusing a dangerous situation when the doors opened again and in walked Gertrude.

'Gertrude.'

'Rachel.'

The sisters hugged each other. While they were thus engaged Gertrude's husband, Alec, sauntered inside with his own crew of hard-eyed gunmen.

10

O'Leary strode across the floor and stood before his daughters, white-faced, and with a visible tremble in his old frame.

'How can you hug this she-devil after what she did to me?' he railed.

The women faced their parent, holding hands and trying to look bemused.

'Father, we're sisters, for God's sake,' Rachel exclaimed. 'What do you want I should do? Pull a Bowie?'

Gertrude shook her head in exaggerated bemusement and turned to her sister.

'Rachel, what a time I've had with Pa and his drunken, ill-mannered oafs. When I tried to restrain them, Pa stormed off in a huff. He said he'd rather spend time with you.'

'Yes, so he said,' Rachel responded with a sympathetic look at her sibling. 'But I've told him I'm not in a position to take him yet. Maybe in the summer. But you're right about his men. They are a bunch of low-lifes.' Rachel turned to her father. 'When you come visiting, just come on your own. It'll be much better all round. I'll be able to take better care of you without that mob of hangers-on.'

'What do you mean – on my own?' The old man's voice was almost a whisper. 'You know I can't venture out alone. There's a price on my head. Have you both gone mad?' He paused for a fraction as if struck by some disturbing thought. 'Or is it me what's mad?'

'There, there now, Pa, that's settled. You go back with Gertrude and leave those good-for-nothings to their own devices.'

'I gave you all,' O'Leary blurted out. 'I gave you my best men and a rich territory to operate in. At one stroke I made you bandit queens. A crew of gunhands so feared that even the law steers clear of us.' O'Leary seemed to shrink within himself. 'My daughter, Catlin – banished from my life. And I am left with . . . she-wolves.'

Abruptly he raised his fists in the air.

'What have I done?' he roared in sudden fury.

The room quietened at the shout. Men watched in silence as O'Leary turned blazing eyes on the two women.

'Bitches – bitches from hell! I curse you. May your wombs be barren! You should give birth only to serpents. Evil will come to those who have congress with such foul devils. I curse you. I curse you both. You are dragons in human form.'

So engrossed were the participants in the drama taking place on the saloon floor that when the roll of thunder crashed above the building, everyone jerked in surprise. It was as if the curses called down by the old man had reached a divine ear and had been answered with the clamour of a fiery storm. The lightning flared somewhere near and the crash of falling shingles echoed through the room.

O'Leary took several lurching steps backwards. His limbs jerked like a puppet being directed across a stage. With a sudden grunt he staggered momentarily and slowly collapsed. For a few moments he twitched on the floor.

Gallagher made a movement to go to the old man's aid. He was stopped by Cornwell's outstretched arm. Before Gallagher could object, O'Leary was clambering back on his feet. He looked around in bewilderment. A white froth had formed on his lips. There was a vacant look in his tired, old eyes. Turning, he staggered to the door and batted his way outside. The rain was just starting to deluge down.

'Looks like a real humdinger of a storm brewing,' Cornwell observed, as he walked to the door and stared out into the rain.

Gallagher hurried across the floor.

'I'll bring him back,' he said. 'God knows what he'll do in that state.'

'Stay where you are,' Cornwell growled. 'Ain't no one going after that old fool. He brought this on himself. Let him go.'

'But . . . the storm. . . .' Gallagher began, but fell silent as the gunman turned a pair of cold eyes on him.

Another roll of thunder crashed overhead. Such was the crescendo of noise some in the room ducked. The torrential rain, assisted by gusts of wind, could be heard buffeting against the walls and windows.

'I said leave him,' Cornwell snarled. 'The old gopher can find a hole to crawl into.'

Gallagher stared into Cornwell's cold, bloodshot eyes. He heard the shuffle of feet behind him as Rachel's men positioned themselves to support their boss.

'I guess you're right at that,' Gallagher said at last and turned back into the room.

Marcus Cogan was standing in the livery staring out at the storm and wondering what was happening up at Gallagher's. He feared for his old boss. He shifted painfully, trying to ease the discomfort of his bruised body. The thunder cracked as he discerned someone staggering through the rain. He gasped as he recognized the man.

'Jeez. . .'

O'Leary blundered inside the livery, rainwater running from his clothing and hat.

'My horse, where's my damned saddle?' he shouted. Seeing Cogan he pointed. 'You there, help me.'

'Mr O'Leary, you'll have to wait till this storm blows over. You can't go out in that.'

'Damn you for an insolent dog. Will no one obey me?'

Cogan watched in consternation as O'Leary grabbed a saddle from a pile and turned back into the storm.

'Damn them all,' the old man muttered. 'Damn them all to hell.'

'O'Leary!' Cogan yelled, but the figure disappeared in the downpour. 'Oh, God,' he groaned as he turned back inside. 'I can't let him go out there on his own.'

The mule was standing placidly regarding him.

'Hecate, I'm sorry for all the harsh things I said about you. I need your help now. We gotta go after O'Leary. There's no figuring what'll happen to him out there all on his lonesome.'

Minutes later, a bemused Cogan led the mule, fully saddled, out into the storm. He had been able to saddle up his mount without the usual wrestling match. He headed in the direction of the corral. As he came around the corner of the livery, he was just in time to see O'Leary urging his mount towards the outskirts of the town.

Such was the force of the storm, in the brief time it took to walk the short distance to the corral Cogan felt that he had trudged through a river bottom. Water was running down his neck and inside his shirt. His boots were filling up as he splashed along.

'Goddamn,' he groaned as he painfully pulled himself into the saddle.

Hunched forward, he set the mule to following the rider as best he could.

'Damn O'Leary and his damned daughters,' he complained as water ran down his face and neck. 'And damn Catlin for being so pigheaded and leaving the old man to the mercy of her sisters.'

11

'I don't like the way things are shaping. I've sent a messenger to Catlin. The sisters are evil. They've only gone and offered a reward for the man who kills O'Leary.'

Monday stared in feigned consternation at his father.

'Pa, surely not. He's their pa for God's sake. Even they couldn't be so ornery.'

'I'm telling you for sure, Monday.' Gallagher's face turned sour. 'Look at Alward. Tries to kill his own pa, murders that Mex girl and attacks his brother.'

'Pa, I don't know. Maybe it was all a terrible mistake.'

'Son, your ma was a whore but look how you turned out. I sure as hell can't figure it. You're the bastard, but my rightful son turns out a wrong 'un. Catlin was O'Leary's favourite and yet he throws her out on her ear without as much as a horse blanket.' Gallagher sighed deeply. 'If I knew where O'Leary was headed I'd take a few supplies to him. The thought of my old friend out in this goddamn storm. . . .'

The saloon owner turned and peered out into the storm-ravaged night and missed the sudden glint in Monday's eyes.

'Pa, I overheard some of O'Leary's men talking. They were to meet up at Mule Back Mine if anything happened to them. I guess it was some sort of backup plan or something.'

Gallagher turned back to his son.

'You sure? Goddamn it, that old man out there. Ain't nothing but a few tumbledown shacks.' He stared at Monday for a few seconds. 'Goddamn it, I got to try and help. He was a good friend to me in the past. Monday, throw a few supplies together. I'm gonna head on out there.'

'Pa, you can't go out in this. Let me go. I'm younger and fitter.'

'You're beginning to sound like your brother – thinking I'm past it, eh?'

'Jeez, Pa, no. I just thought. . . I mean. . . .'

Gallagher gave his son a shove.

'Get those supplies – food and liquor.' As Monday turned away Gallagher called after him. 'Remember, not a word to anyone. Those hellions are itching to kill someone and I guess they wouldn't think twice about shooting me if they thought I was siding with old man O'Leary.'

Not long afterwards Monday watched his father disappear into the rain-shrouded night. The youngster was soaked from being outside in the pouring rain while saddling the horse and loading supplies for Gallagher to take on his rescue mission.

'Mule Back Mine,' he said softly. 'Let's hope you and Al have a troublesome reunion. With a bit of luck neither of you'll survive it.'

Monday was closing the door when he felt the cold hard round of a gun barrel against the back of his neck.

'Half-breed, who was that just gone out?'

'What, I ain't seen no one.'

He heard the click as the gun was cocked.

'Where's Gallagher? Was that him as just left?'

Monday's shoulders slumped.

'Yeah, it was Pa, all right,' he muttered.

'Turn around, breed. I ain't never shot a man from

behind yet.'

Slowly Monday turned round and faced Alec.

'I guess I'd better tell you all,' he said.

'All?' The gunman frowned at the youngster. 'You sure as hell better tell me what the hell's going on.'

'It was Pa as rode out there. He's gone to help that mad, old man, O'Leary.'

The gunfighter smiled thinly without warmth.

'Good boy. You know where he's headed?'

'He wouldn't tell me.'

'Well, in that case, we'll just have to wait for him to return. Maybe he'll bring the mad O'Leary back with him. Should prove fun, don't you think?' The gunman stepped aside. 'You'd better come with me. Gertrude will want to hear this.'

Alec walked the youngster upstairs and pushed him inside one of the bedrooms. Gertrude was sitting at a dressing table, working at her dark lustrous hair. She turned and eyed up the young Gallagher.

She had discarded the black leather outfit. Instead she was dressed in a skimpy underskirt. The revealing garment clung to her voluptuous figure, emphasizing the swell of her breasts and hips. As she swivelled towards the men, they were given an ample view of creamy thighs. A look of satisfaction crossed her face as she noted her performance had the desired effect on the youngster. Monday tried to keep his eyes fixed on Gertrude's face but his gaze kept straying over her profusely sensual body.

'Alec, what have you here?' she asked. 'I'd rather you'd found me a maidservant instead of a soggy pixie.'

'Listen, petal, this soggy pixie has something interesting to tell you.'

Gertrude was examining the rain-soaked Monday with more than a hint of predatory interest. Alec put away the six-shooter and sat on the bed.

'Go on, breed; tell her what you told me.'

'Alec, go and fetch Rachel and Cornwell,' Gertrude ordered. 'They may want to hear this as well.'

The blond man looked surprised.

'Sure, Gertrude,' he said uncertainly. 'Sure thing.'

As the door closed behind Alec, Gertrude came off the chair. She crossed the room in one sinuous movement. Standing close to Monday, he could feel the heat radiating from her body. Gertrude's perfume and nearness swamped his senses.

'Monday,' she purred, her face inches from his, 'they tell me half-breeds have the best attributes of both races. Is that true?'

She reached up a hand and placed it behind his neck. He felt a heady sensation as she gazed intimately into his eyes. As the magnetism of her sex worked on him he lost all willpower. At that moment he would have done anything she asked of him. Her lips met his and a shock passed through his body.

Monday's eyes closed and he lost himself in the intensity of their intimacy. Then she was gone and he was reaching out into a void. His eyes opened and Gertrude was seating herself back in front of the mirror, gazing at her own image. The heat of desire still smouldering within Monday, he could only gape helplessly at the demiurge.

'Now, Monday, tell me everything.'

And he did. He was still talking when Alec arrived back with Rachel.

'Cornwell's out cold – dead drunk – couldn't rouse him,' Alec said and flung himself on the bed.

Rachel eyed Monday and then glanced suspiciously at her sister. Gertrude continued to preen before the mirror.

'Gallagher has gone out to rescue O'Leary,' she said, without turning from her image but watching her sister closely in the glass. 'He has also sent word to Catlin. Told her to come and fetch the old man.' She turned and looked directly at her sister. 'You know what that means? If Catlin comes back and joins up with Pa, they'll try to take over.'

Rachel lit a cigarette as she paced up and down the room.

'We'll have to rally the men and strike before she hits us.' She drew deeply on the cigarette. 'Gertrude, you and Alec get back to Barren Drum and gather as many gun hands as you can muster. I'll wait here for Gallagher to return and try and find out what they're plotting.' She eyed Monday speculatively. 'Where do your loyalties lie in this?'

'Well, he did pass us the information,' Gertrude answered for Monday. 'We may not have known about the plot to bring back Catlin without him wising us up to the plan.'

Rachel smiled intimately at the young half-breed.

'Good, we could do with a loyal soldier in charge here at California Crossing. You get my meaning. You may have to take over from your old pa.'

And Monday smiled back at the blonde woman. Both he and Rachel were unaware of the look of jealousy that flashed from the image in the mirror.

12

There was nothing to see on the bleak hillside, only dim shapes through the sheeting rain. Then lightning would flash and illuminate the old mine workings.

Alward crouched inside one of the abandoned shacks and shivered. He had missed the worst of the storm. The shack was not far from the mine opening where he had hidden his mount. He did not want a chance sighting of the horse to draw unwanted attention. When the storm began he figured Monday would not come out in such weather. He massaged his forehead as he thought over the events of the past few days.

'Xaviera,' he whispered. 'She can't be dead. Who would do such a thing?'

His heart squeezed within him as he saw again her lovely face as she smiled up at him.

'*My beautiful Alward.*'

To distract his morbid thoughts he peered out into the night. But it was no use. Unpleasant images welled up and the youngster was filled with despair. As well as being a suspect for the murder of Xaviera, his pa suspected him of trying to kill him.

'Why the hell should I want to kill Pa? Goddamn it!'

Lightning flashed in one long burst and he saw two riders on the slopes below. He couldn't be sure but they

67

appeared to be arguing. The rain sheeted down and the two men were making no attempt to find shelter.

The youngster had been sitting on old ore sacks. On impulse he pulled them around him – one over his head, another across his shoulders and a third he fastened to his belt like an apron. He went to the door and yelled out at the men. Either they couldn't hear above the storm or were ignoring him. He ran out into the deluge and waved and shouted until they spied him. One of the riders grabbed the other's reins and urged his own mount up the hill towards Alward.

'Quickly, there's shelter in here,' the youngster urged.

He led the men inside the mine opening and watched them dismount. Suddenly he recognized O'Leary. The man with the mule looked like he had taken a battering lately and Alward suspected he was the man who had been beaten by the fat Lovell – one of Rachel's crew.

'You can shelter in the shack,' he said. 'It ain't much but it's out of the storm.'

As the youngster guided them towards the derelict building, O'Leary suddenly stopped. Alward watched as the old man turned his face towards the rain and stood swaying from side to side.

'Boss, come inside out of the rain,' his companion pleaded.

'I'll have none of it – none of it, I tell you,' the old man called out and raised his hands, palms upwards. 'Can you see how the heavens weep? God weeps for poor old fools that give away their possessions to their daughters.' Thunder throbbed overhead. 'You may growl all you like at me, Gertrude; I know your venom well enough.'

Lightning blazed – jagged and bright in the hills above them. The crazy old man clenched his fists and shook them at the sky.

'For God's sake, come inside,' Cogan urged his boss. He

turned to Alward. 'Help me get him inside.'

The youngster moved towards the old man but stopped as O'Leary suddenly screamed out, his face turned up into the drenching rain.

'Why are you raging at me? What have I done to deserve this humiliation? Have my daughters not done enough to me that you too should batter me with your storms?'

'Come inside, Mr O'Leary,' Alward urged. 'We're all getting wet out here.'

The mad old man stared at the speaker then waggled his finger at him.

'You are young, yet. Mark my words, young 'un, never have daughters. They'll throw you out into the wilderness and take everything from you.'

'O'Leary!'

The shout came out of the dark. A horseman could be seen labouring up the slope towards the three men.

'Keane O'Leary,' the man shouted again. 'Thank God I've found you. I've brought you some food.'

As the rider came close, Alward, recognizing his father, pulled the sacking closer about his head so his face was well hidden.

'Gallagher,' O'Leary's companion shouted back over the raging wind and rain. 'Thank God. You've come in the nick of time.'

Gallagher dismounted and holding the reins of his mount, joined the three rain-soaked men.

'I brought you vittles and bourbon,' Gallagher told them.

'Get him to come inside,' Cogan pleaded. 'He's ranting and raving out in this storm.'

Between them the men managed to drag the rambling O'Leary inside the shack.

'Don't take me back,' O'Leary begged. 'I have no daughters now. I'm an old done man. Let me die here.' Suddenly turning to Alward. 'You, fella, you have a fine house here. I'll bide a while with you. Where's my bed?'

'Here you are, sir.' Alward pointed to a pile of sacks. 'You can rest easy. I'll keep watch.'

O'Leary allowed Alward and Cogan to tuck him in the ore sacks. He lay back on the makeshift bed and carried on a meaningless chattering – his daughter's names, Rachel and Gertrude featuring large in his diatribe.

'Who are you, fella?' Gallagher asked Alward, trying to make out his features beneath the sacking.

'I am the voice of one crying in the wilderness,' Alward intoned. 'There is One greater than me. He will come in thunder and rain and wash clean the sins of the world. Repent! Repent! The time is nigh. Are you a sinner, sir? Did you beat your children and cast them out into the dark? Sons and daughters may sin against parents but so too fathers transgress against their children. Is it not written – the sins of the fathers will be visited upon the children for seven generations? Repent! Repent! The kingdom of heaven is upon us.'

'You sound a mite like my dead wife,' Gallagher observed. 'Mind you, there's an element of truth in what you say, though. I had a son. Somehow he went wrong and now he's a wanted murderer.' He turned to Cogan. 'You're the man Lovell near beat to death.'

'Gallagher, I'm Marcus Cogan.'

'What?' The saloon keeper stared intently at Cogan. 'Damn me if it ain't you indeed, Marcus Cogan. What the hell are you doing here?'

'Well, as you may well remember O'Leary threw me out – threatened to gun me down if he saw me again. Hell, I couldn't abandon the old coot. I've been with him too long. So I decided to disguise myself and join up with him again.'

'Marcus Cogan, you're an old fool, but a loyal one at that.' Gallagher shook his head. 'That was some beating you took back there. Dang near came to killing you. Was it worth it?'

'Indeed, I wish Lovell had done a better job of killing me. I'd rather be dead than see O'Leary like this. I love that old man. I fear his mind has slipped.'

'Aye, it's sad indeed. It seems to me his daughters have driven him mad. Rachel and Gertrude have put a price on O'Leary's head. I've sent a message to Catlin to come and rescue him. But it's doubtful if she'll get here in time. As soon as this storm is over there'll be men scouring the country for him. My advice is, if you have any concern for O'Leary's safety, get him out of here and ride like the devil for her ranch. Catlin's your only hope. I'll give you directions how to get there.'

'Thanks, friend. I'll take your advice and get on the road as soon as the storm abates.'

'I'd better get back afore they miss me. The sisters are suspicious of everyone. Such an evil and unnatural pair as I never come across.'

'God go with you, Gallagher. Thanks for the vittles. You're a good friend.'

'Ah, it's little enough. I wish I could do more. But I have my own problems. Good night.'

'Remember, sinner,' Alward screeched after his father's departing figure, 'the sons and daughters of Satan shall find no rest. If you feed your children stones instead of bread they will grind the stones to powder and spew the dust in thine eyes.'

71

13

By the time he arrived back in California Crossing, Gallagher was bone weary. Faint light was visible in the morning sky as the black clouds of the storm moved westwards towards the coast. Wearily he dismounted at the livery. Knowing the old liveryman would be on duty shortly, he left his horse tied up inside the barn. There was a light in the saloon and Gallagher felt a warm glow of satisfaction.

'At least I got one son I can rely on,' he muttered, as he let himself in the back door.

Rubbing his eyes and yawning widely, Gallagher walked quietly into the bar then stopped and blinked in surprise. Several people were gathered inside, seated at the tables.

Rachel lounged back, a cigarette in her mouth, her heels supported on a chair. A few of her gunhands lolled around, drinking or playing cards. Monday was at his usual place behind the bar. Leaning up against the counter was the dark, moustachioed Cornwell. Slowly Gallagher walked to the bar.

'Don't nobody go to bed no more or have you just got up extra early?' he said.

'We've been waiting for you,' Rachel answered.

Looking at O'Leary's daughter, Gallagher was reminded of a snake. Her cold eyes showed no emotion whatsoever as she regarded him through a haze of cigarette smoke.

Gallagher motioned to Monday.

'I could do with a drink.' Whiskey in hand, he turned back to Rachel. 'Thanks, I don't usually have people wait up for me.'

'Where you been, Gallagher?'

The saloon owner frowned at Cornwell who had asked the question.

'Well, I don't think as that's any of your goddamn business.'

Cornwell straightened up from the bar. His hand swung loosely at his side near his holstered gun.

'I'm making it my goddamn business.'

Gallagher sipped at his whiskey which put his hand inches from the gun butt in his shoulder holster. It was an old trick. He would open his fingers and the whiskey glass would slip to the floor while he went for the gun. The distraction of the glass crashing to the floor always worked to his advantage. He had never been bested yet in a shootout.

'You seen anything of my father, lately?' Rachel asked.

Gallagher's eyes flicked back to the woman. She was smiling slightly as she watched him. He noticed the men at the tables had quit their card playing and were also watching him. And then he guessed why they had been waiting for him. Carefully he half turned and set his elbow on the bar. He looked at Monday and gave him the sign. Monday nodded imperceptibly.

They had often worked together like this when trouble loomed. With Monday and his shotgun at his back there were very few situations they could not handle. The gun came into his hand slick and fast. It caught Cornwell by surprise. The bandit's hand was on his gun but with Gallagher's weapon aimed at him, he did not draw.

'Now,' Gallagher said casually, 'as a matter of fact, Rachel, I did see your pa. I saw a pathetic old man weeping his eyes out 'cause his daughters had thrown him out like a piece of worn-out carpet.'

Still watching Cornwell out of the corner of his eye, the saloon owner turned his attention to Rachel.

'Your father is no threat to you. Between you and Gertrude, you kicked the heart out of him. I watched that broken old man rave like a demented loon. That didn't sit too well with me. I want you and your husband, Cornwell here, to pack your belongings and leave my place. You've wore out your welcome as far as I'm concerned. You're no longer welcome.'

'You son of a bitch,' Cornwell muttered thickly.

'What about Catlin, Gallagher?' Rachel asked.

As she spoke, Rachel reached inside her mink jacket and Gallagher tensed. But instead of a weapon she produced a gold cigarette case. Extracting a slim cylinder, she extended an arm. Obediently one of her gunnies scratched a sulphur head and held it for her as she sucked on her tailor-made cigarette. Blowing a cloud of blue smoke, she gave her attention back to Gallagher.

'Well?' she said, smoke drifting from her mouth and nose. 'I'll ask you again: what message did you send to Catlin?'

'Can't say as I know what you're talking about. What's Catlin got to do with any of this?'

'I was thinking you might have financed her for her goddamn ranch she and Frank hankered after. So that being the case, if you and she joined together, you would make a formidable force with her wranglers and your town gunnies. You might just be tempted to help her move against Gertrude an' me.'

'Jesus wept! You're as crazed as your old pa. Where'd you get such foolish notions? I've had enough of this. I've told you once. Now I'm telling you again. Pack up and get on out of here. Monday!'

Monday obediently lifted the shotgun from below the

bar and swung the barrel against his father's head. As the saloon owner sagged to his knees, Cornwell pulled his own revolver and in a couple of quick strides, was at Gallagher's side. But even as he did so the stricken man pulled the trigger.

Cornwell yelped and went back against the bar with the bullet lodged in his abdomen. Monday smashed the shotgun once more against his father's head and Gallagher collapsed on the floor. The wounded Cornwell aimed his revolver at the unconscious man.

'Don't kill him!' Rachel screamed. 'We got to find out what he was planning with Catlin.'

When Gallagher came to, he was sitting in one of his own chairs. Cords were wound around his body, securing him in place. Dazedly he looked around him. Cornwell was also sitting, holding a blood soaked wad of cotton against his abdomen. With her usual cigarette, Rachel was standing by her husband's side.

'Hell kite, Rachel, this hurts,' Cornwell moaned.

'Just hang on,' Rachel reassured him. 'We've sent for the sawbones. He'll patch you up.'

'I need a drink.'

Rachel motioned to Monday and Gallagher saw his son carry a half-full whiskey bottle to the wounded man. Cornwell put the bottle to his mouth. In spite of his dazed state Gallagher spoke out.

'Shouldn't drink on a gut wound.'

The bottle upended as the wounded man ignored him.

'Ah,' Rachel observed, 'you're awake.' She moved to his side. 'We need to talk, you and I.'

Gallagher ignored Rachel and glared past her at Monday.

'You,' he gritted, his voice bitter. 'It was you as took a shot at me, weren't it? It weren't Alward, at all. Why? What'd I ever do to you?'

Rachel blew tobacco smoke in the saloon owner's face. Gallagher blinked as his eyes watered.

'He did it to get his rightful inheritance,' she said. 'You should have stepped down like O'Leary did. But you're too dumb for that. You old timers have had your day. This business needs youngsters like Monday and myself. Your time is over. Anyway, that's not important. What I need right now, is to know what you were plotting with Catlin.'

'Go to hell,' Gallagher said bitterly. 'You poison everything you touch. Your pa was right. You and your sister are she-devils.'

'Tut-tut, you stupid old man,' Rachel said, and very casually she pushed her cigarette into Gallagher's right eye.

Gallagher screamed loudly. He screamed at the sudden bright pain that filled his head.

'Aaaagh!'

He trashed about in the chair, moaning loudly. Rachel walked back to her table and lit another cigarette. She looked over at Monday and winked at him through the fresh smoke. He looked back at her, the glow of admiration in his eyes. Gallagher was shaking his head from side to side, moaning like an animal in distress.

'Oh God, my eye, my goddamn eye. What have you done, you bitch? You've about blinded me, you goddamn whore.'

'Gallagher, now that you see we're serious, I'll ask you again. What are you and Catlin up to?'

'Go to hell!' Gallagher yelled. 'Go to hell, you and all your goddamned family. And take that whoreson, Monday with you. I never want to see him ever again. Oh God, oh God. My goddamn eye.'

Gallagher lapsed into low moaning.

'What?' Rachel asked amiably. 'You don't want to see your son anymore? Well, I can fix that. Yes, Gallagher, I can tell you now, you'll never lay eyes on that handsome son of yours again.'

Rachel drew deeply on her cigarette. The burning tip was glowing almost white as she took it from her mouth. With that same casual unconcern she pushed the incandescent ember into Gallagher's remaining good eye.

It was done so unexpectedly Gallagher had no time to blink. His head jerked backwards and his screams rung through the bar room. So extreme were his tortured convulsions his chair overbalanced and he crashed to the floor.

The screams went on and on. Monday was gazing at his father with a rapt expression. Cornwell was trying to smile through his own discomfort. Rachel's men were shifting uneasily in their chairs with looks of discomfort on their faces. She turned to them.

'Untie him and sling him outside.'

Men moved to do her bidding and Gallagher was pushed out through the doors, alternatively cursing and shrieking. When the men returned, Cornwell was stretched out on the floor, his eyes open in the fixed stare of death. Rachel was bent over him. None of them saw the stiletto she slipped inside her clothing. Rachel looked up at Monday, hovering nearby.

'Looks like we both got rid of some unwanted baggage today,' she remarked casually.

'You're sure one goddamned hellcat,' Monday observed. 'I'll never be able to sleep easy in your bed again.'

Rachel rose and wound herself round the half-breed.

'I'll damn well make sure of that.'

Outside, the sound of moaning faded as the dispossessed saloon owner, with burnt-out eyes, stumbled and fell – stumbled and fell – his progress painfully slow along the muddy street of California Crossing.

14

Cogan, his face still swollen and bruised, shook the dozing youngster awake.

'Preacher, we're getting ready to head out. You wanna join us?'

During the night O'Leary's ranting had prevented any real sleep. Cogan had believed the ramshackle shanty would not last the night but in spite of the battering it had taken from the wind and rain, it was still standing.

'I . . . I must stay here,' Alward replied. 'The Good Lord has told me to await the coming of my brother. We will ride out together and preach against the sins of the world.'

'Look, son, why don't you come with us? I'm sure there'll be plenty of sin where we're going. They'll be glad of some preaching.'

The youngster pulled his sacking closer around him.

'You will ride into the valley of evil,' he intoned, still keeping to his role of wandering preacher. 'Death shall be your companion. Do not put your trust in the will of men. They are full of corruption. Follow the Lord in all things. Do not fornicate. Do not steal. Do not kill. Do not swear false oaths. All these evil practices will condemn you in the eyes of the Lord.'

Cogan sighed. 'I guess you could be right at that, Preacher.'

He abandoned his attempt to persuade the youngster to accompany them.

'I'll leave you some grub. I can't leave much, but it'll maybe do you until this deliverer of yours comes. There's plenty of water about after all that rain. Good luck, fella.'

'God make your paths straight and your way strewn with sweet blooms,' Alward said. 'I will pray to the Good Lord for your safe deliverance.'

O'Leary was standing in the doorway staring out into the night. The rain had virtually ceased and heeding Gallagher's warning, Cogan was preparing to move out before any of the daughters' gunmen found them.

'You got your gun handy, fella?' O'Leary suddenly queried.

Cogan tensed and fingered the butt of his revolver, thinking the old man had seen someone outside.

'There's a gold shipment they're sending down through Moulder Pass,' the old bandit chief continued. 'It should be coming through at first light. You take the east side and I'll hit them from the west wall.' He stepped outside. 'Don't make a move until you hear my signal. I'll hoot like an owl.'

O'Leary gave a passable imitation of an owl. Cogan followed the old man outside. O'Leary kept up his hooting. Once or twice Cogan tried to hush him but it was no use. The hooting continued. So preoccupied was he with perfecting his owl hoots that it took all of Cogan's efforts to get the old man on his horse. He had to almost lift O'Leary into the saddle. His own body was a mass of throbbing pain. His face was stiff and aching and he wondered where the overblown Lovell was right now.

'I just hope I meet you without your devilish mistresses to protect you,' he muttered. 'We'll see what you're made of then, you cowardly lard pudding.'

Cogan was still bemused by the docile behaviour of his new mount. Ever since he had crawled into the stables, more dead than alive and the mule had stood over him protecting him and licking his wounds, it had been a model companion.

In spite of this, Cogan was deeply suspicious of the apparent change. He still exercised extreme care when approaching the animal. As he saddled and bridled the beast, he was forever on the alert for a sly attack on his person.

'I can't figure you, Hecate,' he told the mule. 'I guess you're plotting something dire. I only wish I knew what it was. And,' he added wryly, 'I sure as hell hope I'm not around when you try it.'

To the accompaniment of owl hoots, the two men rode away from Mule Back Mine. Cogan was alert for signs of pursuit. He kept casting around the landscape for a sign of riders out hunting them. They rode on a goodly way without spotting anything suspicious. About mid-morning, O'Leary ceased his owl impersonations and rode in quiet contemplation.

Cogan, still weak from his beating and lack of sleep, found it hard to keep his eyes open. Time and again he jerked his head up after snoozing for a few moments in the saddle. He looked at his companion. O'Leary's eyes were closed as his lips moved in soundless nonsense.

'We got to stop and have a rest, boss,' Cogan said. 'Otherwise I'll topple off this here mule and break my neck. Mind you, with all these here aches and pains I'd probably not notice.'

The old man smiled vacantly but made no reply. Cogan sighed, and looked around for a likely place to stop. They had gone about a mile further when he saw a giant cottonwood that had obviously fallen during last night's storm.

'Should give us cover for a while,' he told his companion. 'We'll rest awhile here.'

There was no response. They dismounted and Cogan

settled the old man among the foliage of the fallen tree. O'Leary kept up a muttered diatribe.

'Stay put, boss,' Cogan told him. 'I'll be right as rain in a while.'

He curled up on the damp ground and was asleep immediately.

Cogan groaned as Lovell, with an evil leer on his face, kicked him again and again. The pain was brutal and real.

'Goddamn you, I'll kill you this time, you bastard,' Cogan swore and tried to kick back.

'Wake up, you mad asshole,' a voice insisted.

Pain seared through Cogan's side as a boot thudded into his damaged ribs. He groaned and opened his eyes. Two gunmen were standing gazing down at him. Groggily Cogan shook his head and looked around.

Apart from the mule, that seemed intent on munching its way through the downed cottonwood tree, he was alone with two sadistic gunmen. There was no sign of O'Leary or his horse. Another kick and another agonizing bolt of pain.

'We're looking for O'Leary. You're that cockroach as tried to kill Lovell. Where's that crazy old loon O'Leary?'

'For God's sake stop kicking me,' Cogan yelled. 'How do I know where he is? I'm heading for the gold diggings. I've had enough of the O'Learys to last me a lifetime. I'm getting out.'

The tall lean character with the week's stubble on his cheeks kicked Cogan again. His victim tried to roll with the kick but was too slow and the boot caught him in the spine. Cogan arched his back in agony.

'Oh, God, this hurts too much.'

A gun barrel slashed him across the back of the head and he saw stars. When the lights had settled in his head, the men were still there, patiently waiting an answer.

'Mister, we can beat you senseless. It'll take time but we'll enjoy doing it. Now, where's O'Leary?'

In spite of the odds Cogan went for his gun and slapped an empty holster.

'Is this what you're looking for, you sad bastard?'

The second gunman held up Cogan's revolver. His face was pockmarked as if he had been ravaged by disease at an early age.

'You know something, fella?' Cogan groaned. 'Things started going wrong when I had that haircut. I guess I shoulda heeded that fella, Samson in the Bible. His story went something similar. He had a haircut and everything went wrong after that. Only instead of Samson and Delilah it's Marcus and Hecate.'

'Cut the crap, lug head. What did you do with that old bastard O'Leary?'

'Believe me, fellas, I wish I could help, but I don't know a thing about O'Leary. The last I saw he was in California Crossing. Ouch!'

The last a grunt as the taller of the two booted him in the face.

'Goddamn!' Cogan moaned as warm blood trickled from a pulpy nose.

He buried his face in his hands and curled up in a ball. The man with the pocked face hunkered down beside him.

'Look, make this easy on yourself. Just tell us what we want to know. We ain't gonna hurt the old fool. We was told to bring him in so as he could be cared for.'

Cogan peered through his hands at his tormentor. The man was toying with his gun – spinning it on his forefinger. At intervals the spinning would cease and the barrel would be pointing at the man on the ground. Cogan winced every time that happened, expecting each time the gunman would pull the trigger.

'Please, fellas, believe me. Please, I just started working for this O'Leary fella. I ain't got no loyalty to him. I just want out with a whole skin.'

'You'll share in the reward.'

Cogan looked expectantly at Pock-face.

'Reward, you mean there's a reward for this O'Leary?' he asked. 'I didn't know about no reward. Maybe I can help you after all.'

Cogan sat up, trying to look interested and wondering if he could snatch Pock-face's gun and turn it on the two men. The odds were not great for the success of such a move but his options in the situation were very limited, very limited indeed.

'You see, Jordan.' Pock-face grinned up at the lean man. 'Sprinkle a little gold dust and everyone's your friend all of a sudden.'

The man called Jordan screamed. His face turned white and he rose up on his toes and flailed his hands helplessly in the air. Pock-face gawked up at his friend. He began to stand and Cogan kicked him between the legs and made a grab for the six-shooter.

While Jordan screamed for his friend to help him, Cogan and Pock-face wrestled on the ground for possession of the gun. The gunman head-butted Cogan and he almost lost consciousness. Only a desperate desire to stay alive kept him fighting. The gun went off abruptly and the bullet ploughed into Jordan's abdomen. The gunman gave a strangled, gurgling sound and keeled over on top of his companion, blood seeping from the bullet hole.

'Goddamn it, Jordan! What the hell. . . ?'

Cogan sunk his teeth into the man's hand and he yelped and let go of the gun. The gunman kicked and fought as he tried to get out from under the collapsed Jordan and at the same time fend off Cogan.

'You goddamn piece of cow dung,' he raged. 'You just shot Jordan.'

That he had fast reactions were evident. While Cogan fumbled to get a grip on the disputed revolver, Pock-face abandoned the struggle and grabbed for Jordan's gun instead. He swivelled back and turned the Colt on Cogan. Cogan went very still.

'Drop it, you goddamn bastard. I'll blow your goddamn head apart.'

Cogan allowed the weapon to fall from his slack fingers. He stared helplessly at the nozzle of the gun just a few feet from his face. The gunman scrambled to his feet.

'Jordan, goddamn it, Jordan,' the gunman yelled, staring down at his companion.

His hand was shaking so much he had to use both hands to hold his gun steady. When Jordan did not answer, the gunman screamed obscenities at Cogan.

'You killed my goddamn partner, you bastard.'

Cogan might have pointed out the gun that killed Jordan was in Pock-face's hand when it went off but thought now was not the time to dispute the point. He sat on the ground, awaiting the shot that would finish him.

Let it be quick and clean, he prayed.

'Bastard,' screamed the gunman as he cocked the weapon.

He never got to fire it. Large, yellow canines closed over his wrist. Jaws that had been shredding branches of cottonwood crunched down on bone and gristle. The gunman was screaming as his arm was reduced to minced flesh and splintered bones.

He went on his knees, still screaming. The gun fell from fingers suddenly deprived of nerves and blood. Only then did the mule release the mangled arm and step back. Blood pumped in scarlet streams from the hideous wound and on to his dead companion.

Cogan stood up with the discarded gun in his hand. He did not raise it for he reckoned neither of the men posed a threat. The mule had backed away and now stood facing him. That wicked grin was on its face.

'Hecate,' Cogan whispered, 'I . . . I. . . .'

He paused, lost for words. There was a moan from the injured man.

'Help me.'

He was staring pathetically at Cogan. Blood was still pumping with slightly less vigour from his lacerated arm. There was blood on his companion, blood on the leaves of the cottonwood and blood on the injured man's clothing.

'Help me,' the wounded man said again in a faint voice.

Cogan contemplated the blood-soaked surroundings.

'That's a terrible mess you're making. I hope you're gonna clean up after. You know how hard it is to get blood out of clothing. Your friend's just soaked in the stuff.'

The wounded man did not answer. He had keeled over in a dead faint, his chewed up arm slowly leaking blood into the dirt. It was only then Cogan noticed the huge rip in the backside of Jordan's pants. Blood and faeces had run in streams down the man's legs.

Cogan turned and looked at the mule. Hesitantly he walked over to the beast. Slowly he reached out and placed his hand on the broad forehead. The mule ignored him and carried on munching leaves. Cogan stroked the rough grey head.

'Goddamn, son of a bitch. You saved my life, you goddamn son of a bitch.'

Cogan went on stroking. The mule turned its head and gazed up at Cogan. He stared into big violet eyes, poised to leap out of range of those deadly teeth. The mule snickered enigmatically then went back to chomping leaves.

15

When O'Leary and his companion departed the shack, Alward wrapped the dank-smelling ore sacks around him and tried to sleep. But sleep was as elusive as it had been during the night when O'Leary's mad rambling had kept him awake.

He wondered what had happened to drive the old man to such a state. From the conversation between his father and Cogan, he had learned that the old man had had an altercation with his daughters.

Alward remembered the O'Leary women, and their hard-bitten and arrogant husbands. He had met them at the jamboree they had attended in honour of O'Leary's retirement. The women had seemed too sophisticated and calculating for Alward's taste. He liked his women soft, compliant and loving.

'Xaviera.'

He spoke the name softly. An empty feeling overwhelmed him and he left the corner where he had been resting and walked to the door. The youngster stared out into the darkness. The storm had passed and left in its wake a light rain. Hot tears spilled down, trickling into the stubble on his cheeks.

Alward Gallagher was trying to come to terms with the fact that his life was changed forever. The young, carefree dude was now a destitute saddle bum. All the things he had enjoyed in the past were lost to him forever: his love trysts with Xaviera, his comfortable life back in California Crossing, his father and brother.

At last he stifled his sobs, rubbing the tears from his eyes, unconsciously smearing grime on to his face and beard. The elegant young fop from California Crossing was, bit by bit, being effaced, and a grubby hobo was gradually taking his place.

'Monday, where the hell are you? I need to know what's happening.'

Remembering the horse Monday had lent him, he made his way into the mineshaft and led the animal out and around the back of the shack. There was grass growing there and he hobbled the horse near a water trough brimming with rainwater. He stood watching the animal feed for a while before retracing his steps around the front of the shack to resume his lonely vigil.

The daylight was well advanced with the sun struggling to break through thick cloud when he spotted movement on the slopes below. He did not change his position for he was inside the doorway of the shack and could not be seen.

There were two riders and he watched as they made their way up the trail. Their progress was slow and torturous to watch. As they drew near he could see a lead rope between the two riders. Alward could not imagine who it was coming up to the old deserted mine, needing to lead someone. He began to wonder if this was indeed Monday or someone else altogether. There was nothing to do, only watch and wait. Then he recognized the leading rider.

It was Charlie Turley, the oldster who ran the livery stable. The puzzling thing was the identity of the rider trailing behind. As far as Alward could make out, the man was blindfolded. He pulled the sacking close around him and stepped outside.

'Halloa there,' Charlie called out to the hooded figure.

'The Lord gives and the Lord takes away,' replied Alward in a high pitched chant. 'Repent your sins now and the Lord will forgive. All those who seek forgiveness will not be driven from the face of the Lord. . . .'

Alward's voice trailed away. It was only now he recognized the man on the second horse. He forced himself to continue.

'Repent, you sinners, repent. The day of judgement will soon be upon us.'

The riders pulled up. Alward ceased his ranting and stared at his blindfolded father.

'That must be the preacher fella,' Gallagher said.

'I guess so,' Charlie replied. 'No sign of anyone else, though.'

'Preacher, what happened to the two men as were here last night?' Gallagher asked his son. 'Have they moved on?'

'Aye, they departed in the night,' Alward said. 'I know not where they went.'

'Thank God at least for that. Maybe they'll be safe.'

The youngster stared in some distress at his father. He needed to know why he was blindfolded.

'How did you sin, my friend? Are you hiding your eyes from this world of shame?'

Charlie Turley climbed down from his mount and went to assist Gallagher.

'His eyes was put out, Preacher. O'Leary's hellcat daughter did it. I weren't there to see it myself. Maybe he'll tell you himself what happened.'

'His eyes. . .'Alward's voice faltered, then remembered his role. 'A hellcat you say? Has the gates of hell been broken down and the denizens allowed to roam the streets? Was there the smell of brimstone at her appearance?'

Gallagher, with Charlie's help, had dismounted by now. It was he who answered Alward.

'It was not brimstone but tobacco. O'Leary's daughter, Rachel stubbed her cigarette out in my eyes.' He touched the rough bandage covering his eyes. 'Charlie here looked after me. Put some liniment on and bandaged me.'

Charlie guided the blind man towards the shack.

'It was ointment I use on the horse's eyes when they get sore. I guess it won't do no harm to use it on burned eyes. Should be all right in a day or two.'

The oldster shook his head in a negative manner while passing his hand across his own eyes. They reached the door of the shack. Alward could only stare helplessly at his bandaged father. He ached to reach out and touch him but was afraid to betray himself.

'Hast the Lord gave him no children to assist him?' he asked instead.

'Children!' snorted Gallagher. 'Hah! My own son betrayed me. My own son!'

'The children of Beelzebub go without shame on the streets,' Alward wailed. 'When the Lord comes he will blast them into the everlasting flames of hell. Woe to all sinners, for on that day, which will be the end of days, the wrath of God will be great.'

'Come here, Preacher,' Gallagher said.

Alward moved close to his father. The blind man reached out and touched his son's face, running his hand over the stubble and grime.

'I remember you from last night. I had a son once. He would have been about your age. I treated him wrong. Drove him from me. The son I took to my bosom betrayed me. Now I have no children. I am like O'Leary now. One child betrayed and one child fled.'

Alward turned to Charlie and shrugged his shoulders, at the same time indicating with his hands that he was at a loss to understand what Gallagher was talking about.

'He has two sons, Preacher,' the oldster said. 'One a

breed – a bastard by a squaw. The other was his natural son. The half-breed joined forces with the O'Leary females and helped blind him. No one knows what happened to Alward, his other son. There was some trouble over a Mex girl. That's all I know.'

'Preacher, if I tell you the way I want to go, will you guide me?' Gallagher intervened. 'I need to follow those two men who were here last night. I know where they are headed but I cannot find the way on my own. Will you be my eyes?'

'Your son betrayed you,' Alward whispered. 'Surely that cannot be true? Blood is thicker than water.'

'It's true, Preacher. My son, Monday, delivered me into the hands of that she-devil, Rachel. She put my eyes out with no more thought than she would stamp on a beetle. Will you help me? My way is long and dark.'

'I will go inside the temple and pray for guidance,' Alward answered. 'Perhaps it is the Lord's will that I become your staff. Bide awhile. I must parley with the Lord.'

Inside the dim hut, Alward sat and stared at the rectangle of light that was the doorway, his head a confusion of emotions. Monday's betrayal was almost as great a shock as was the blinding of his father. Alward sat there, trying to get his mind around the crazy turn of events and could make no sense of any of it. He stared hopelessly into space as he listened to the two men outside.

'What's the preacher fella doing now, Charlie?'

'He's gone inside the shack. Guess he must be praying. What you going to do now? Were you banking on finding them two fellas here?'

'It doesn't matter that they're gone if the preacher will be my guide. Those two men were O'Leary and an old friend. His name was Cogan. He had been a scout for O'Leary before his daughters took over.'

'Where was this fella Cogan taking him then?'

90

'When O'Leary threw out his youngest daughter, Catlin without a cent, it was me as gave her a stake. She wanted to set up a horse ranch in Nevada. Had a place all sorted out, but when her father disowned her, that looked like the end of her plans. Then I stepped in and staked her and her man. They went ahead and bought the ranch. I own a part share in it. That's where I told Cogan to take O'Leary. Figured he would be safe there. Now I need a safe haven myself.'

'Well, you'd better hope God's on your side and allows that preacher fella to help you.'

Alward stepped back outside again.

'I will lift up mine eyes to the hills and become a beacon to those in darkness,' he intoned. 'Come, poor eyeless one. I am to be your guide. I shall be your staff to lean on in the days of travail that lie ahead. We will become pilgrims and journey through the valley of darkness.'

'Well, I guess that solves your problem, Gallagher,' Charlie Turley observed. 'Looks like this preacher fella's going to take you on after all.'

'Aye, these are strange times when the blind are led by the mad. But that, it seems to me, is the way of this world.'

16

Barren Drum was a hive of activity. Riders were constantly coming and going. In the past when O'Leary needed men, he had recruited them in much smaller numbers. This was the first time in living memory such a large band of men had been assembled for a job. The nature of the business in hand was secret, which was only to be expected in an outlaw community. Spies and informers were everywhere and a job could be compromised if details leaked out.

In the midst of this anthill of activity, Gertrude sat in a room inside the main house. While preparations for the raid went on she sat naked before her mirror and brooded. From time to time she touched her hair or angled her face in an effort to observe her profile.

'I know he found me attractive,' she murmured.

She placed her hands beneath full breasts and gently moved them up and down. Her nipples had been further enhanced with rouge. She pursed fleshy lips and looked coyly at her image.

'When I kissed him I could feel his excitement as we touched. I know he wanted me.' Her eyes narrowed. 'Rachel has been very cunning. She sent me here to be out of the way so she could have him to herself. I know that bitch.' Suddenly she giggled. 'She is a frail sister.' Sobering again, she stared hard into the mirror. 'My heart constricts to think of my erring sister and Monday together. She shall not have him. He is too young and innocent for the likes of her to blight.'

Further ruminations were interrupted by a knock on the door.

'Who is it?' she called.

'Lovell, madam. I'm back.'

When she opened the door to the underling, she was dressed in a silken robe that revealed more than it covered. Lovell stared at his mistress with his slightly bulging cow's eyes.

'Ma'am. . .' he stammered as she held the door wide and gestured for him to enter.

'What news?' she asked tartly, as he shuffled self-consciously into the room

'It's all good, ma'am. They captured the traitor Gallagher. He refused to confirm what Monday had told. However, Rachel took Monday's word over Gallagher. She thinks Gallagher sent your father on to Catlin's ranch. Rachel has men out looking for O'Leary. He should be taken soon—'

'How was my sister?' Gertrude cut in sharply. 'How was she with Monday?'

'They were on very good terms, ma'am. He helped her when she burnt out Gallagher's eyes.'

'Burnt out his eyes?' Rachel exclaimed. 'My sister excels herself. And Monday helped her. What was Cornwell doing while this was going on?'

'Before he was taken, Gallagher shot Cornwell.'

'What! My sister a widow! And alone with Monday.'

As Rachel turned away from Lovell, the door opened and Alec walked in.

'Bad news about Cornwell,' he remarked, as he closed the door behind him. 'I hope this don't stop Rachel. We need men who can rally behind her.'

'Apparently not,' Gertrude replied nonchalantly. 'It seems she has recruited a new ally in Monday.'

'The breed!' Alec nodded thoughtfully. 'As long as he has the backing of Gallagher's crew it sounds like a shrewd move. It looks as if the information he passed on about Catlin and Frank was on the up and up.' He shook his head in admiration. 'Rachel sure covers all the angles.' He missed the venomous look his wife darted at him. 'In that case we should move out in the morning. If we don't give these rannies something to do soon, they'll start fighting amongst themselves.'

Alec turned to the portly messenger who was trying to look anywhere but at his mistress.

'Lovell, do you know where Rachel is at now?'

'Sure, boss, her and Monday are taking the trail towards Nevada and Catlin's horse ranch. Rachel sends word she won't do nothing until you come up and join her. You're to rendezvous at Matador Chimney.'

'Good, I've drawn up a plan of action. You get over there and tell Rachel we're on our way. Tell her we should have close to thirty men. . . Oh, hell, I'll write it all down with the rendezvous and all. That way you won't leave anything out. Be ready to ride shortly.'

Alec turned abruptly and left.

'Ma'am.'

Lovell nodded obsequiously to his mistress and turned to follow Alec.

'Wait,' the woman ordered.

Gertrude went to a chest and sat writing a note. She sealed it and turned to the fat man.

'Can I trust you, Lovell?' she asked.

'You have my life on it,' he swore.

'This note is for Monday. No one else must see it. I don't trust Rachel. I worry she has some other agenda in mind. I need to know what she is plotting. This note should get me

94

some answers. But no one – I repeat, no one – must see this. It is for Monday's eyes only. Is that clear?'

Lovell took the note and pushed it inside his shirt.

'I am your trusted servant, ma'am. I would die for you.'

And looking at the voluptuous woman before him, at that moment Lovell almost believed his own avowal.

17

The large herd of horses was hard to keep together over the rough terrain but Eulitereo Cardinalle was proud of the way his vaqueros worked them. The order for the horses had come from a ranch up in Nevada just over the border with California.

Right now he was looking for a suitable place to bed the herd down for the night. Though it was still early he was growing uneasy as he observed a mass of dark clouds out to the east. Eulitereo knew a thunderstorm was heading in their direction. There was a possibility it would pass them by, but he could not take the risk of a bad storm spooking the horses. He signalled to his head vaquero, Felipe Manola, a burly young man with a thick black moustache that made him look older than his twenty-two years.

'Storm coming, boss,' Felipe called. 'We need to find a safe place for the night.'

'Ride on ahead, Felipe,' Eulitereo told him. 'See if you can find somewhere to sit out the storm. Can't have the herd spooked this late in our drive. Another day should bring us to our destination.'

'Sí.'

Felipe spurred away and Eulitereo cast another anxious glance at the dark horizon. Felipe located a narrow draw within a few miles and Eulitereo drove his precious herd inside and posted riders to keep the horses contained.

Sometime during the night the storm hit. Thunder roared and the lightning lit up the sky. Rain pounded on sombreros and equipment, making it difficult to see anything. It took the best efforts of Eulitereo's men to contain the frightened horses. When morning came and the storm drifted off towards the east, the men were exhausted and the horses agitated and skittish.

'We'll rest up here until midday,' Eulitereo informed his weary vaqueros. 'Give us a chance to recover. By then the horses won't be so jumpy. They'll be somewhat easier to handle. All that rain has given them plenty to drink and maybe we'll find pasture later today.'

With a few men riding herd, the remainder of the vaqueros lounged around the campfire, taking it easy and recuperating from a night of hard riding. It had been a fraught several hours while the storm raged around them. The vaqueros had worked hard making sure the herd did not become frightened and bolt. Now they relaxed and smoked and drank coffee and talked amongst themselves.

It was about mid-morning when they heard the racket. Men lifted their heads and listened. Strange echoing cries drifted down the arroyo. The vaqueros looked at each other and frowned. Eulitereo walked to the edge of the camp and stared in the direction from which the eerie wailing was coming.

'This place is haunted,' someone suggested.

And indeed the strange noises seemed not of human origin. The wailing rose and fell and the men glanced uneasily at each other. Even the horses were becoming restless. A few of the *vaqueros* crossed themselves and fingered religious emblems strung within their clothing.

'It is someone singing,' Eulitereo decided.

Around him his men inclined their heads as they listened. The words came fluttering down the draw and the *vaqueros* listened to the lament of the singer.

> *Of all the poor fools who inhabit the earth,*
> *Fools by misfortune, or fools from their birth,*
> *Rich fools and poor fools, and great fools and small,*
> *The man who has daughters is the greatest of all.*

As the singer hove into sight and perceived the camp he ceased his song. He walked his mount right up to the fire.

'Have you stuck the hog, fellas?' he asked.

'Hog?' Eulitereo queried, looked puzzled.

'You don't light a fire without a hog to roast.'

The man snorted several times in imitation of the animal he had mentioned. The vaqueros stared curiously at the newcomer. He had leafy sprigs tucked into various parts of his clothing. They looked like cottonwood leaves. The skin of his face was stretched like rawhide and deeply etched with age lines. The man climbed stiffly from his horse and squatted by the fire.

'I had daughters once that served me coffee,' he said, and looked slyly at Eulitereo. 'Do you have daughters?'

Eulitereo shook his head. 'No, *señor*, I have two fine sons.'

'Very wise. Very wise.'

The man nodded his head then looked around as if to make sure no one was close enough to overhear his next remark.

'My advice to you is to drown daughters at birth. Otherwise they'll grow up with sharp nails and pointed teeth.'

The old man stared pensively into the fire and then softly began to sing again. Seeing the man was distracted, Eulitereo poured coffee and handed him the mug.

'You have lost your daughters, *señor*?'

The stranger took the proffered mug and stared vacantly

into the distance. Not answering Eulitereo's question, he continued his soft chanting once more.

'I think he's mad,' whispered Felipe.

'I don't suppose you have squirrel?' the old man said suddenly. 'I do have a hankering after roasted squirrel. Mind you, take only the young 'uns. The old 'uns are tough. Their daughters make them like that.'

The *vaqueros* were looking fearfully at the stranger. To their superstitious minds, madness was associated with satanic possession. Some were marking the cross on their torso while others were making the protective sign against the evil eye. Eulitereo reached across and gently urged the man to drink the coffee.

'Are you hungry?' he asked. 'What is your name?'

For answer the stranger took a twig from his pocket and began scratching in the earth.

'My name is writ in dust. The wind will blow and I will vanish along with my name. I have no sons, you see. My wife gave birth to vixens. They lashed me with their sharp tongues and tossed me out into the storm.' He looked shrewdly at Eulitereo. 'Did you ever think why God did not have daughters? He only had a son, you see. God is all wise. He knew about daughters – Jezebels and Magdalenas.' Suddenly he frowned. 'Herod had a daughter. She couldn't get a boar's head so she had John the Baptist's head instead.'

The old man nodded pensively. His listeners were spellbound, listening to his foolish talk.

'I've ate muskrat. Bit like chicken that was. You sure you got no squirrel?'

Eulitereo shook his head. 'No squirrel, old man. We got beans and tortillas. You're welcome to that.' He nodded to the cook. 'Give him a helping of beans, Juan. Then make ready to move out.' He stood up. 'OK, fellas, siesta over. Time to do some work.'

As the men bustled about packing away the camp, Felipe pointed to the old man, still seated by the fire, taking no notice of the activity around him. The plate of food was held limply in his hand. He was making no attempt to eat.

'What about him? We can't leave him like this. Perhaps the madness is only temporary. Will we take him with us? If we leave him I don't think he will survive.'

'You're right, Felipe. Get one of the vaqueros to tie a lead rope to his horse. Mebby we'll meet someone who knows who he is.'

When the herd set out again one of the vaqueros led the madman's horse. The strange, foolish old man seemed quite content to be guided along. And he never tired of singing his song of fools and daughters, repeating the same verse over and over.

18

'You got a gun, Preacher?'

Alward looked back at his father with a frown on his face. He was leading the blind man's horse and had been lost in contemplation. Ever since his father had told him of Monday's role in putting out his eyes, he had been agonizing over the happenings of the last few days.

'Guns are the instruments of Satan,' he said. 'The devil invented gunpowder for Cain to murder his brother. All men who bear guns are children of Cain.'

In truth Alward was weary of the deception but he was not sure how to bring it to an end. He worried his father might still harbour ill-will against him and was working on some way of revealing his identity without too much trauma for the blind man. After all that had happened to his pa, Alward could sense he was teetering on the verge of a breakdown.

The treachery of two sons and the vicious blinding were brutal blows. Also, from being an independent businessman to a blind beggar was one hell of a fall. Alward wasn't sure how the old man was coping with his drastic change of fortune.

'I take it that's a no,' Gallagher said dourly. 'What if we're attacked by bandits or Apache?'

'The Lord is my guide and protector, blind one. Do not

fear to put your trust in the Lord. Faith is my shield and trust is my spear.'

The truth was that Alward did not have any weapons. When he had fled from California Crossing he had ridden out without even a shirt on his back, so insistent had been his brother Monday's urging. All he had, if it could be called a weapon, was the cutthroat razor he had been about to use when he was interrupted in his ablutions. Alward had stuffed it in his pocket before clambering on Monday's horse and fleeing the vengeful Mexicans. Anxious to find out his father's feelings towards himself, he began to quiz him.

'Can you find forgiveness in your heart for your sons?'

'Humph!' the old man snorted. 'You tell me, Preacher. I took Monday into my confidence about Catlin and her man. Told him I had sent word to her and was hoping to find O'Leary and send him on to her. He spilled all that out to Rachel and Cornwell. Then he busted my head with the shotgun. When Rachel burned my eyes he made no move to help me. You tell me, Preacher – should I forgive him?

'Now I'm riding round the country with a dumb-ass, holy peculiar and you think I should forgive my bastard son and thank him for his betrayal? I ain't that kinda man. I tell you this – if I could find someone as would put a bullet in Monday's brain and then finish me off, I'd gladly give him everything I owned. My own son. . . .'

At that point Gallagher's voice trailed off.

'You mentioned you had two sons,' Alward remarked as casually as he could. 'Was he as bad as this here Monday fella?'

'Huh, Alward? I bin thinking about Alward since all this happened. It was Monday as found Alward's knife in the alley and planted it in my mind it was him as was gunning for me. Then Alward runs and Monday is found rolling about in the alley with a knife cut. Said as Alward had cut him and stole his horse.'

'He cut his own brother!' Alward exclaimed.

The pieces were beginning to come together for the youngster. The extent of Monday's perfidy was stunning. Monday with a set of cunning devices had succeeded in exiling his father and brother. In a well-planned coup he had dispossessed the Gallagher family. Unless Alward was mistaken, Monday was now in charge of all the Gallagher assets in California Crossing.

'The bastard, bastard by name and bastard by nature,' he cursed with some feeling.

'What's that, Preacher? You see something ahead?'

'No, no, I was just praying for your bastard son, is all.'

'Pray he gets leprosy. I curse the day I whelped him. Through him I lost my son and my eyes and my living. And now tell me again, Preacher, as I should forgive him.'

Father and son lapsed into silence then, each lost in his own bitter reflections until they were hailed unexpectedly by a rider coming up on them.

'Hello there, fellow travellers.'

Alward was jerked out of his ruminations. He looked around to see a horseman coming up behind them. Horse and rider were covered in trail dust, evidence of hard riding. Alward reined in and waited while the man caught up with them.

'This sure is a lonely trail, fellas. You're the first travellers I've come across since I started out this morning. I'm kinda lost. Wonder if you can point me in the direction of Matador Chimney? I think this north-westerly trail is the right one but I would feel more comfortable if you fellas could confirm the location.'

By now the man was alongside them and was looking askance at Alward's unkempt appearance.

'We follow the Lord's path, my friend,' Alward told him. 'I do believe this road will lead at length to Matador

Chimney. If you care to accompany us we are not averse to company.'

'No, thanks, fella.' The man looked Alward up and down with evident distaste. 'I'm particular who I travel with. Can't abide saddle bums, for sure. You smell like you crawled outta a coyote's asshole.'

'My friend,' Alward replied, trying to curb his anger at the man's contemptuous tone, 'I have been washed in the waters of Babylon. Though my outer raiment is of the grime of this earth, my soul shines with the holy light of the Lord. Bide a while and pray with us.'

'Shove your prayers up your filthy ass. I hate all preachers and the like. If I weren't in such a hurry I'd stop and give you a thrashing, blasted god-botherer! In fact I've a mind to put a bullet in your head just for the hell of it—'

'Hang on there, stranger,' Gallagher interrupted. 'That ain't no way to talk to a man of God. He ain't done nothing to harm you. Ride on your way and leave the poor preacher fella alone.'

The man wheeled his mount about so he faced towards the blindfolded man. Suddenly he went still. A slow smile stretched across his pudgy face.

'Well, well, well. By all that's holy. Look what we got here.' He swivelled his head back towards Alward. 'Maybe there is a god after all. He sure as hell's done me a favour today.'

Alward watched the man carefully. He had no idea what he had in mind but he was obviously a bully. Finding a preacher and a helpless, blind man alone on the trail had sparked off some cruel streak in that mean breast.

'Pass on, friend, I will pray for you. The Lord does not abandon sinners. You will find forgiveness. . . .'

But the man ignored him and was dismounting. He walked over to Gallagher's mount and took the reins in his hand.

'Of all the people in all this godforsaken country I should meet, it would be you, the traitor Gallagher. This is my lucky day indeed.'

'You know me, friend. How come you know me?'

The man's smile grew broader.

'I was there when Rachel put out your eyes. She let you go but the half-breed told her it was a mistake so she ordered you killed. Even put a price on your miserable old head.'

He drew a Bowie from its sheath. It looked long and deadly in his chubby hand.

'I guess I'll take your scalp back as proof I killed you.' Suddenly the big man laughed out loud. 'Learned to scalp from an old buffler hunter.' He turned back to Alward with a twisted grin. 'You watch this, Preacher. Scalping's an art. The scalp has to be peeled – you don't cut it off. Similar to skinning a rabbit.'

'Leave him be, friend. Pass on your way. We want no trouble.'

Alward spoke in his normal tone. Gone was the preachy tone of the madman he had used since taking charge of his blind father.

'Get down off that horse, Gallagher. This is gonna hurt a mite but then you'll be dead and all your troubles will be over.'

'Willingly, friend, willingly. I offer my neck to the knife. Do what you like with me. I have no wish to live. Along with my eyes I have lost everything I ever held dear.'

Gallagher slid down from his horse and stood submissively awaiting his fate. The stranger knocked the old man's hat from his head. Gallagher's grey locks looked dank and pathetic on his sweaty head. He bowed towards the stranger as if inviting the stroke of the knife. The man with the Bowie reached out and gripped him by the ear.

'Stop that!' Alward shouted, climbing down from his

horse. He approached the two men. 'This has gone far enough. Get on your way, stranger.'

The man leered at Alward.

'Preacher, I ain't got no quarrel with you. Just you stop there and watch a professional bounty hunter at work. Always bring back a trophy. A scalp is a kinda decoration as a man can show off to let people know he's got balls. When the O'Leary women find out it was me, Nolan Lovell as killed Gallagher, I'll rise in the ranks. Maybe even get into Gertrude's bed.' His laugh was slightly hysterical. 'Now, wouldn't that be something.'

Alward snatched at the man's sleeve.

'No. Leave him be!' he yelled.

Lovell swung the Bowie and slashed it across Alward's chest. The youngster jerked back as the blade bit into the sacking he wore as part of his disguise. The thick material prevented the blade from doing any damage.

'Goddamn you, Preacher, you're dead.'

Lovell let go of Gallagher and turned his attention to Alward.

'Preacher, it's all right. Let him do his work,' Gallagher called out. 'It will be a mercy for me to die. I have nothing to live for. There's gold in my saddle bags. Take it and build yourself a church. Put my name on the floor of the entrance hall so that people can trample it underfoot as they go in and out. You can write, in memory of Gallagher, a blind old fool.'

Alward was backing away from the knife. At the mention of gold his attacker paused. His brutal face twisted into an avaricious grin.

'Gold. Who could have foretold such good fortune for Nolan Lovell when he set out from Barren Drum this morning? I will have Gallagher's gold as well as the reward for killing him. Now Preacher, are you gonna run or have I gotta stick this Bowie in your worthless guts? I'd as soon kill you as well as this old blind coot.'

While the man was talking, Alward pulled the sacking from his shoulders. As he backed away, he wrapped the material around his forearm. Lovell laughed in scorn.

'You think that'll save you, Preacher. Look, I'm doing you a favour. I would be sending you to your maker. You'd think a godly fella like yourself would be grateful.'

Lovell suddenly lunged forward. Alward leapt to one side. He was hoping to get around behind his horse. But the beast shied away, leaving him still exposed. The knife-man laughed.

'I ain't never stuck a preacher afore. Maybe you want to sing a hymn or something. My old pappy got religion. Used to beat me every day with a fence rail. Said as he was beating the devil out of me.

'He would recite psalms as he raised the lumps. Let me see now. What psalm shall we have for you, Preacher? You got any requests? I know most of them. My pappy insisted I learn them off by heart so as I could recite them with him as he beat the living daylights out of me.'

As he talked the fat man was stalking Alward. They were circling warily. Lovell was confident. He was not expecting any resistance from a preacher and a blind man. He would stick the preacher, scalp Gallagher and take the gold he had in the saddle-bags.

19

The horses breasted the brow of the hill and milled around, unsure which direction to go. Smelling the sweet grass and water, they poured down the hill in a dark tide. The Mexican drovers hemmed them in on both sides and kept the leaders from bolting.

In the distance could be seen the low buildings of the ranch. Eulitereo urged his mount into a gallop past the outside of the herd. He waved to Felipe to let him know he was riding on to the ranch.

'Keep 'em tight,' he yelled but doubted if his second in command heard him.

It did not matter. Felipe was an experienced vaquero and Eulitereo knew he could count on him to keep the herd under control. As he rode towards the ranch he noticed a small group of horsemen advancing towards him. Eulitereo kept on going, wondering if this was a welcoming committee come to help bring in the herd.

The group of riders and the lone horseman met about midway between the herd and the ranch. They pulled up when Eulitereo raised his hand in greeting. The riders milled around as he approached. He was surprised to see they were all heavily armed with side arms and carbines.

'Eulitereo Cardinalle,' he called out. 'I've brought the horses that were ordered. I'm looking for Frank Carter.'

A young woman nudged her horse towards him.

'*Señor* Cardinalle, I am Catlin O'Leary. Frank isn't here at the moment.'

Eulitereo studied her. He saw a handsome young woman gazing at him with serious brown eyes. He swept his sombrero from his head.

'Greetings, *señorita*, it is a pleasure to meet you. Where can I hold the herd while I wait for *Señor* Carter?'

She turned to one of her riders.

'Tim, you go with *Señor* Cardinalle's men,' she told him. 'Take them down by the creek. They can water the horses and then let them graze on the north pasture.'

The rider cut away from the group and rode towards the herd. Catlin turned back to the Mexican.

'You have caught us at a bad time, *señor*. If you and your men would make yourselves at home, we will be back shortly.' She hesitated a moment before continuing. 'I am sorry, *Señor* Cardinalle, you have come a long way. You do need an explanation. My father is missing. Frank has gone out to look for him. Since then I have had more serious news. Some people are hunting him. It is too complicated to explain it all to you now. Will you be patient and wait for us?'

Eulitereo shrugged. 'I am sorry for your trouble, *señorita*. I understand you must help your father. We will camp by the creek and await your return.'

As he finished speaking someone hailed him. He turned to see one of his riders approaching. It was the *vaquero* assigned to look after the madman. Eulitereo waved the rider forward. He was trailing the lead rope. The madman was slumped in his saddle, his face obscured by his hat. Eulitereo turned back to the woman.

'We found this poor fella wandering alone out there. He. . . .' Eulitereo hesitated and touched his finger to his forehead. 'He is not quite right in the head. For his own safety we brought him along. I did not know what else to do. I could not leave him.'

The *vaquero* drew alongside. He tipped his hat to Catlin then looked enquiringly at his boss. Eulitereo turned back to the woman. She was staring past him. Her face had gone quite pale.

'Father?' she said in a voice that quavered somewhat. 'Father, is that you?'

Then she was off her horse and reaching out to touch the old man's leg.

'Father,' she said again.

He raised his head slightly and opened his eyes.

'Who calls me father?' he said his voice quavering. 'I have no children. When children have no parents they are called orphans. What do you call a parent with no children? You call him an old fool.'

'Father.' She pulled at his trouser leg. 'It is me, Catlin.'

'Catlin. I did have a daughter once by that name. But she is dead now. Soon I hope to join her.' He frowned suddenly. 'It rained last night, Catlin. I have done wicked things in my life but I never . . . never. . . .'

His voice trailed off. He reached down and touched Catlin's hand resting on his knee and peered intently into her face.

'Are those tears in those soft eyes? Are you angry with me? If you have poison for me I will drink it. Your sisters abused me. They threw me out in the storm. I would not have treated my enemy's dog as they misused me.'

'Father, come back to the house with me.' Tears were indeed coursing down Catlin's face. 'You're safe now. I'll take care of you.'

Swiftly Catlin issued instructions to her riders. They wheeled their mounts and set off back to the ranch. At last she turned to the Mexican.

'*Señor* Cardinalle, I am in your debt. This is the man we

were looking for. It is my father and he has gone through some troubled times. I will take him to the house and care for him. When you have seen to the herd I would like you to join us. We will have supper together and settle up our business.'

Eulitereo raised his sombrero and inclined his head.

'I am happy for such a good ending.'

Eulitereo watched while the girl took the lead rope from the vaquero. She mounted her own horse and slowly headed back to the ranch trailing her father's horse. The Mexican shook his head thoughtfully.

'There is much sorrow and mystery in this, Juan,' he said to the vaquero. 'The madman spoke of his daughters abusing him and yet when he meets this woman she calls him father and is most tender with him.' He reined around his horse. 'Come, let us join Felipe and the herd. Perhaps I will learn more when I come to dinner with this handsome woman.'

20

'I have a fit psalm for you, Preacher. I want you to join in,' Lovell told Alward. 'I'm sure you'll know it. *My God, my God, why hast thou forsaken me? Where art thou when I cry for help? I cry in the day and I call out in the night.* Preacher, you ain't joining in.'

The large blade flashed in the air. Alward dodged but felt a blow on his upper arm as the knife sliced into him. Desperately he back-pedalled and the knifeman laughed harshly. Blood was weeping down the youngster's arm.

'*My father trusted in thee and didst deliver me onto you. His fists were granite and his boots iron. My bruised body cried out for vengeance.*'

Alward saw his father moving towards them, his hands outstretched as he groped blindly towards the noise of conflict.

'Stay back, Gallagher,' he yelled.

Lovell glanced over his shoulder and Alward saw his chance. He flung himself forward. Out of the corner of his eye Lovell saw him move. The knife came round in an arc and Alward stumbled to the ground, blood pouring from a long gash in his chest. He was trying to scramble out of range on all fours when Lovell kicked him in the side of the head.

Lights exploded in the youngster's head and he blacked

out for a moment. When the world stopped spinning he was conscious of a weight pressing down on his body. He looked up into the corpulent face leering down at him with discoloured teeth exposed in a taut grimace.

'Now where shall we start to cut, Preacher?' Lovell taunted.

The knife swished back and forth – bright and sharp. Alward's hypnotized eyes followed the glittering movements. His hands were trapped by his side beneath Lovell's heavy thighs. He felt a hard object pressing into his own thigh and realized it was the razor he had been about to shave with when Monday had hustled him outside.

That had been the start of his nightmare. He wondered if it was all to end now with this fat bastard carving bits off him. His father would be next as the bounty hunter took his scalp to claim the reward. Lovell put the point of the knife against the corner of Alward's eye.

'Maybe I should take out your eyes, Preacher.'

The point dug in. It took all Alward's restraint not to scream. Slowly and deliberately the knife was drawn down his face. The flesh parted on each side of the keen blade. Blood ran down the youngster's face and pooled in his ear. Lovell put his head to one side as he contemplated his work.

'The fillies don't like scars,' he said, nodding with satisfaction. 'When you get to paradise the houris might just reject you. Shall I do a matching line on the other side, Preacher man? Eh, what do you think?'

The knife dug into the flesh on the left side of the youngster's face and Alward did scream then.

'You goddamn, fat, lousy bastard.'

The youngster tried to wrench his head away but this only caused the blade to cut down across his cheek and slice into his earlobe.

'Goddamn you, Preacher!' Lovell yelled. 'Look what you

made me do'

He slashed the bloody blade down across Alward's chest, cutting from the shoulder in a diagonal stroke to his nipple. With the gash already inflicted, an X was now carved on Alward's chest.

The youngster convulsed and writhed beneath the crushing weight of his tormentor. It was a futile struggle. The fat man grinned down at him and then drove the haft of his Bowie into Alward's mouth. With his other hand he backhanded the youth, deliberately hitting him on the gaping gash in his cheek.

Alward gagged and coughed as blood from his mashed and cut lips trickled back into his throat. He spit out blood and Lovell laughed. The smile vanished as a pair of brawny arms closed around the fat man.

'What the. . . .'

Through a haze of pain Alward felt the weight of his tormentor lift from him. He blinked as he saw the blindfolded face beyond the cursing twisted features of Lovell. The fat man thrashed about, trying desperately to free himself from the arms clamped tightly around his chest.

Alward groaned. Then he thrust his hand inside his trouser pocket. He felt the slim shape of the razor. He knew exactly what he had to do.

Lovell's struggles had taken the two men a few feet away. Alward managed to make it to his knees and shuffled forward. As he moved he was unfolding the razor's blade from its ivory handle.

It had been an expensive instrument, made of best steel and sharpened to a keen finish. Alward had been stropping the edge prior to shaving before Monday had interrupted him and bid him flee the Mexicans baying for his blood.

Lovell saw him coming – the open razor in his hand. The fat man's eyes widened in fear and his struggles became more frantic. But Gallagher was a physically powerful man.

His arms were clamped tightly around the bounty hunter. Gallagher had locked his hands together and nothing was going to loosen his grip. Big as he was, there was no way Lovell would be able to break that hold.

The fat blowhard struggled wildly and yelled out all sorts of threats and curses. The more Lovell thrashed about the tighter Gallagher gripped, those rigid arms clamped around his chest like the metal bands around a beer cask.

'Run, Preacher,' Gallagher called. 'I'll hold him long enough for you to get away. Take my horse. It has the gold in the saddle-bags.'

Lovell stared in horror at the bloody figure shambling towards him. Alward's face was a mask of blood. His lips were drawn back in a snarl of pain as he stumbled towards the grappling men.

Blood streamed from the deep slits in his cheeks. His teeth were covered in blood that dribbled down his chin, transforming his grimace of pain into a bizarre grin of death.

'*Thou turnest man to destruction and sayest, return ye children to the killing fields,*' Alward intoned. '*Thou carriest them away in blood.*'

'Run, Preacher,' Gallagher called again.

'*They are as killer wolves,*' Alward ground on relentlessly as the blood poured from his hideous wounds. '*In the morning your shadow passes over their graves. Their blood shall water the earth.*'

His hand reached out and gripped the fat man's shirt. The razor came up and Alward stroked hard across the thick neck. Lovell opened his mouth to scream. Blood suddenly pumped out from the ghastly wound in his throat and jetted on to Alward. The youngster tried to back away from the spouting blood and wondered at the heat of the stuff as it poured onto his arms and chest. Suddenly he did not care and collapsed into the dirt and lay there watching Lovell's dying struggles. Even as the blood drained from the dreadful wound in his neck, Gallagher, unaware of what had happened, still held the man upright.

'It's all right, Pa,' Alward called. 'You can let go now.'

Slowly Gallagher relaxed his grip. The dead man slid through his arms and collapsed onto the dirt.

'You called me Pa,' Gallagher said. 'I thank you for that, but I ain't fitten to be no one's pa.'

'It's me, Pa. Alward, your son, come back to haunt you.'

'Alward, Alward . . . is that really you? What happened? Where did you come from?'

'It's a long story, Pa. I'll tell you later.'

'Oh, Alward, is it really you? My boy, my boy.'

Gallagher was groping towards the youngster, homing in on the voice.

'Don't touch me, Pa. I'm covered in blood.'

But the questing hands had found the youngster and moved to his face. Alward winced as his father's hands stroked him, touching the dreadful gashes inflicted by Lovell and increasing the pain of his ruined face.

'Oh Alward, is it really you? Oh, my boy. Can you forgive me, son? I believed that snake, Monday and you had to flee. It's all my fault.'

The old man's voice broke and he began to sob.

'It's all right, Pa. It weren't your fault. Monday fooled us all. Now sit by me. I must bind these wounds.' He glanced at the dead man. 'I can use this fat bastard's shirt.'

Painfully he moved across and using the razor, he hacked away the man's vest and then cut away his shirt. As he worked some papers were dislodged. He set these to one side and cut the shirt into strips, which he painstakingly bound about his face. The makeshift bandages were soon soaked in blood but he hoped the flow must soon stop.

Picking up the letters, he moved away from the corpse and examined the papers. One was addressed to Monday and the other bore Rachel's name. Quickly he tore open the one for his brother and began to read.

'My God, brother Monday works fast. He's wormed his way in with Rachel and now it looks as if Gertrude has the hots for him as well. She wants him to get rid of Alec so he can take his place.'

The next letter detailed plans for the O'Leary sisters to join forces and attack Catlin's ranch. Carefully Alward folded the letters and set them to one side.

He had taken no notice of his father as the man crawled across to the body of Lovell and continued the search Alward had left off. He had only been interested in utilizing the dead man's shirt and the letters had fallen out as he had cut away the material. When the youngster looked up he went very still. His blind father had found something much more sinister.

'Pa,' he said quietly, trying to keep his voice from quavering. 'What are you doing?'

There was a grim smile on the blind man's face as he knelt beside the bloodied corpse of Lovell.

'I'd be a burden to you, Alward. It's better this way.'

'No! No, Pa, not that!'

In spite of the pain in his much-abused body he flung himself forward. He was too late – much too late by a long margin. The shot blew out the rear of Gallagher's head. The blind man toppled backwards. The gun slid out from between his teeth as the hand that held it slackened its grip.

'Pa, goddamn it, Pa, I would have looked after you.'

Alward cradled the body in his arms. He stared in horror at the mass of bone and blood that had been his father's head and tried to hold back the bile that rose in his throat. For what seemed an age he sat there, rocking back and forth, his father's body cradled in his arms; hot tears mingling with the blood on his lacerated face.

When he could stand, Alward took the big Bowie knife

that Lovell had used to butcher him and dug a grave for his father. It took him a long time. Loss of blood and shock had enfeebled him. With his father interred, he used the razor to cut holes in the ore sacks and fashion a crude jacket. He stowed the letters in the saddle bags. The gold was there just as his father had said. Lovell's pistol and Bowie knife and the razor he hid inside his crude clothing.

Alward roped the two spare horses together and climbed on board his father's mare. Then he set off, trailing the spare horses and looking like a survivor from a bloody battlefield.

Lovell's body lay bloated and obscene. The youngster had not thought it fitting to bury the bounty hunter near his father's grave. Instead he left it to be devoured by whatever wild beasts happened upon it.

'Rest in peace, Pa. I will find that viper Monday and we will have a day of reckoning.'

21

Alward lay on the hillside and watched the rider on the trail below. As the man sat his horse, he could see the stranger was viewing something through a scope. From his blind father's directions he knew he was close to Catlin's horse ranch.

Climbing back on his horse, Alward continued down the trail towards the silent watcher. As he approached he made no attempt to conceal his presence. The man with the telescope snapped it shut and turned to watch the approaching rider, his hand resting on his sidearm. It was then that Alward recognized him. He had seen him on the arm of O'Leary's daughter Gertrude and remembered his name was Alec.

'May the good Lord bring His blessings upon you and your family,' he called, raising his hand in greeting.

Alec made no reply as he watched the youngster approach. Alward wondered what he must think of the strange, bloodstained figure approaching.

The crude binding cut from the dead Lovell's shirt and wrapped around his face had finally stopped the bleeding. But not before the material had become soaked in blood. Along with the bizarre face bandages there was his coarse outfit fashioned from ore sacks.

'Let the peace of the Lord shine His blessings upon you,'

Alward continued in the face of the man's silence.

His face felt hot and stiff and painful. The knife wounds on his body also burned agonizingly, making every movement a pain-wracked effort.

Alward kept his hand raised in greeting. With his other hand engaged in holding the reins of his horse, he reasoned he would not appear in any way threatening. The effort of riding this far had taxed his strength. It made him weak and dizzy and he had to make a real effort to keep upright.

'What happened to you, fella?' Alec asked. 'You been head-butting cactus or what?'

'The Lord was angry with me. Out of the night He spoke to me. His voice was terrible to behold. He told me I must atone for my sins. The Lord commanded me to scourge my body. So I mutilated the things that had brought me onto the sins of the flesh.'

Alec reached up and pushed his hat to the back of his head, exposing his blond hair.

'What the hell sins did you commit? Musta been something a mite severe for you to cut yourself up like that.'

'I committed the sin of darkness with my mistress. I went into her bedroom at night while her lawful husband was away and we dallied in shameful deeds. My face was my temptation. Now no woman will look at me with lust ever again. I will live in the desert with wild beasts as my companions.'

A grin spread across the blond gunslinger's face as he listened to this declaration.

'I've met some crazy folk in my time but you are the craziest son of a bitch I ever did come across in a long time.'

Alward pulled out the letters he had found on Lovell and pretended to study them.

'I have one last task to perform before I commit myself to the wilderness. It was a dying man's last request that I

120

deliver these letters. I have to find these people. One letter is addressed to someone called Monday and the other is called Rachel. Perhaps I will find someone in the next town or settlement that may be able to help.'

He looked up at Alec and saw the smile had faded from the gunman's face.

'Let me see those,' he snapped.

Alward willingly handed over the letters.

'Perhaps you recognize the names?' he asked.

Alec paid him no attention. He was busy examining the letters.

'Gertrude's writing,' he mused.

There was a few minutes' silence as he read. When he finally looked up at Alward his face had gone taut. His eyes had taken on an icy hue.

'You read these notes?' he asked, his voice tight.

'No, indeed I did not, friend. I do not pry into people's private business. I read only the good book. I try to find solace there. The writings of man have no substance for me. . . .'

Alward trailed off. Alec had wheeled his horse past him and was urging it back down the trail.

'Methinks mischief has been sown amongst the enemy,' he said softly as he watched the departing gunman.

He turned back to the trail and saw what the blond man had been watching through his eyeglass. In the far distance was a set of low buildings. Alward nudged his horse forward.

'Pa,' he muttered. 'I think I might have arrived at Catlin's ranch. I certainly hope so, for I am sore in mind and body and could do with lying down and sleeping for a month of Sundays.'

Sometime later as he neared the ranch he was challenged by an armed lookout. When Alward told him he had urgent news for Catlin he was waved through. The man who answered his knock on the door looked askance at the new-comer.

'What the hell, fella? You stuck your head through the spokes of a buggy wheel while it was still turning? Come on in.'

A dark-haired, young woman came out of a room and blinked owlishly at Alward.

'Howdy, Miss Catlin. I'm Alward Gallagher.'

She frowned at him. 'Gallagher's son! What happened to you? Where is your pa?'

'He's dead, ma'am. I buried him today. I was bringing him here when we were attacked and Pa was killed.'

Another man came into the hall. Alward recognized Cogan, who had been at the old mine-shack with O'Leary.

'Did I hear you right?' Cogan asked. 'Gallagher dead . . . killed?'

Alward nodded and then leaned wearily against the wall as exhaustion swept through him. Cogan moved swiftly to his side.

'You look in a bad way, fella.'

'Take him in the kitchen, Marcus,' Catlin said. 'We'll get Frank to patch him up.'

'No time, ma'am. Your sisters are coming,' Alward managed to say before he sagged against Cogan.

'Go on, Marcus,' Catlin urged. 'Take him through. I'll come as soon as I find Frank.' She turned to Alward and said in a gentle tone, 'You can tell it all then.'

The process of removing Alward's makeshift bandages was painful and time consuming. As Frank Carter worked on him, he tried to tell as much as he knew of the impending attack on the ranch.

'The letters I took off the dead messenger mentioned a gathering of men to make up an attacking force. Gertrude and Rachel are teaming up with Monday. I think when all these riders are in place, they intend to attack the ranch. I don't know if the alliance will hold, for I managed to pass the letters to Alec. The one from Gertrude to Monday was very explicit. She wanted Monday to get rid of Alec and for her and him to take over.'

At that stage he passed out. When he came too, Carter was using a needle and thread to sew his cheeks together. Alward about passed out again. Cogan held a whiskey bottle to his lips.

'Get that down your neck, kid.'

Alward gulped convulsively. The raw liquor burned its way into his stomach. He did his best to empty the bottle. It had very little effect in dulling the pain.

'Never saw anything like it. There ain't nothing I can do about the scars,' Carter mused as he sewed. 'You're gonna look like hell. What happened to the fella as cut you?'

'I slit his throat,' Alward slurred his words, whiskey and weariness overwhelming him.

'So you was that mad preacher boy,' Cogan stated. 'Even your own pa didn't recognize you.'

Alward said nothing. The memory of the last few days was too painful. His head was whirling and he slumped back in the chair. The voices went on around him but muted as if coming from a long way away. He just wanted to sleep and then he remembered Monday and more than anything else he wanted to meet up with his brother.

22

Catlin looked with some pity on the mutilated young man who had found his way to her ranch.

'He's out for the count,' she said. 'Carry him out to the bunkhouse and bed him down.'

Between them, Marcus Cogan and Frank Carter carried the unconscious Alward from the kitchen. When the two men returned, Catlin was staring out the window. She turned around to gaze at her partner, noticing how done in he looked.

Frank rubbed a hand across his face and left a smear of blood on his cheekbone. Catlin picked up a piece of cotton and came across and wiped his face.

'The longer he sleeps the better,' Frank told her. 'I don't know how he'll feel when he wakes up and gets a sight of his ruined face.'

'We'll have to leave him sleeping it off out there in the bunkhouse for now,' Catlin said. 'We have done our duty by him. His father was a good friend to us. We can repay the old man by looking after his son.' She sighed deeply. 'Gertrude and Rachel are our main worry. It looks as if they'll have gathered a small army out there. Any time now they'll be coming down out of the hills to attack us.'

Frank placed his hands on her shoulders and gazed earnestly into her face.

'We should ride out now – go somewhere well away from that evil family of yours.'

'I . . . I can't, Frank. Father's not fit to travel. I won't leave him. And nor is poor Alward. We can't leave them. After all that has happened, they would just slaughter Pa and in all likelihood that young man you just patched up.'

'That's what I figured you'd say. In that case we'll just have to fight.'

Frank turned from her and stared moodily out at the surrounding country.

'Will the Mexicans help?' he asked.

Catlin nodded. 'I think so. Cardinalle came to dinner last night and I told him most of what was happening. He offered to hang around for a couple of days in case I need him and his men.'

Marcus Cogan had remained silent as this exchange was taking place. Now he spoke up.

'I could ride out and scout around,' he offered. 'Try and find out what's happening. Maybe give you warning when they start to move.'

'Thank you, Marcus. You've been a good friend.' Catlin gave him an appraising look. 'You look much younger now without those whiskers—'

'Take a fast horse,' Frank interposed. 'You'll need a good mount in case they spot you and you have to run for it. I'll organize things here. I think the best thing is to hole up in the ranch. They'll have to come at us and we'll be under cover. Send someone for the Mexican. Tell him we're expecting an attack anytime. We can spread them round the barns and outhouses. I just hope they can shoot.'

When Cardinalle rode into the yard, Catlin and Carter greeted him and told him of the impending action. The Mexican cast a professional eye around the buildings. He nodded.

'The ranch is defendable, but it would be bad strategy to concentrate all your forces in one place. Some of my men, like me, are ex-cavalry. If we conceal ourselves down by the creek, when the assault comes we can ride around the perimeter and harass the attackers. Caught between two lines of attack they might think they have bitten off more than they can chew and fall back. Once they do that you can move your men out from the house and press home an attack. Often when men are on retreat they sometimes keep on going. We push and push and push and *madre dios*, they break and run.'

Frank looked at the Mexican for a few moments before replying.

'I sure wish I had your faith.' Then he shrugged. 'We've sent a man out to scout around. He may be able to warn us when the attack will come. My belief is that it will come sooner rather than later.'

'Sí, señor, I will go and prepare my men. They will be glad to help. I would like to think you will continue ranching here and I can sell you many more horses.'

Catlin and Frank watched the Mexican ride away. They turned back to the house. Both stopped and stared at the gaunt figure in the doorway.

'Father, should you be out of bed? You've been very ill.'

As she spoke Catlin moved up beside the old man. His white hair hung in untidy strands and his gaunt face had a waxen look.

'Don't try to bamboozle me, Catlin. I heard everything. Are they coming? Are Gertrude and Rachel coming for me?'

Gone was the distracted look of the insane. The bloodshot old eyes gazed wearily at his daughter.

'Yes,' she said simply.

His eyes clouded and he shifted his gaze to stare moodily into the distance.

'I have brought much trouble upon my family. You especially, Catlin, have I wronged. My other daughters are vipers. If you will ready me a horse I'll ride out and give myself up to them. Perhaps that will satisfy their deranged and unnatural rancour. You and Frank can live on here in peace.'

'I'm an O'Leary, Father,' Catlin retorted. 'You are my family. I will not allow you to fall into the hands of my wretched sisters. And do you really think they would stop once they have you? You should know better than that. They will either kill you or use you as a bargaining chip to make me give in to their demands. No. You will stay here and we will defeat them. They are fighting a lost cause. And if Alward is to be believed, their own jealousy and spite might just defeat them.'

The old man stepped out into the yard. He ran his eye around the outbuildings.

'What have you got that'll burn?' he asked.

Frank furrowed his brow in thought.

'We got a few barrels of kerosene. Had fresh supplies in last week.'

O'Leary stalked around the yard, estimating distances and angles.

'I notice you have a bow hanging in the parlour,' O'Leary said at one point. 'Is it just for show or can you use it?'

'It's mine,' Frank said. 'An Apache gave it to me when I cured his child of fever. I sometimes practice with it. Why?'

O'Leary eyed him for a moment.

'You'll have to let me have a free hand and lend me some of your men. We gotta prepare for a siege and I got some ideas of how to go about it.'

'O'Leary, we've had our differences in the past,' Frank said. 'But I believe in letting bygones be bygones. You go ahead and do whatever you have to do. I bow to your greater experience in these things. I'm only a humble horse doctor.'

O'Leary gave back a tight smile.

'Just show me where the kerosene is at,' he said.

Eulitereo Cardinalle sat on a fallen log. Beside him, the river bubbled and splashed pleasantly. It was this creek that made the site of the horse ranch such a desirable location. His head vaquero Felipe was watching him with an earnest look in his face. They were obviously in the midst of a serious discussion.

'I promised the woman I would help defend her ranch,' Eulitereo said at last.

'This is a gringo war, Eulitereo. We only contracted to deliver horses – not to fight in their battles,' Felipe pleaded.

'What do you suggest, Felipe?'

'I say we ride. We ride for home. Let the gringos slaughter each other. Will your men thank you for taking them into a war not of their making? With the odds as they are, how many of us will survive? What will be easier to live with – breaking your promise to the gringos or watching your vaqueros being massacred in a foolish conflict?'

'*Madre dios*, Felipe, when you put it like that it does not leave much room for manoeuvre.' Eulitereo sighed heavily. 'Tell the men. We ride out immediately.'

Felipe rose, but hesitated.

'What about the herd, Eulitereo?'

Eulitereo eyed his second in command.

'What about the herd?' he asked.

'Should we not take it into safekeeping? After all,' Felipe shrugged expressively, 'it would be a pity if it fell into the wrong hands or perhaps it might be left with no one to claim it.'

His boss shook his head.

'You know, Felipe, it is a good job you did not become a bandit. You make a very dishonest *vaquero*. OK, round up the horses. We will take them to a safe place.'

23

The rank smell of kerosene was strong in the air. By the time O'Leary had finished his preparations the two barrels of fuel had been used up. The barns and outhouses were strewn with straw soaked in the stuff. Roofs were doused in kerosene and soaked rags stuffed around the base.

O'Leary strode through the area directing and instructing the hands in the work. Gone was the deranged old man and in his place the bandit chief was taking charge.

'I think they'll just swoop down on the ranch and hope to overwhelm us by force of numbers,' he told Catlin. 'At first we'll defend the outhouses as far as possible. If the attackers prove too strong our men will fall back to the main house. It's a good stout building and should withstand an attack. Your sisters' men will naturally take over the barns and snipe at us from there. When they are well entrenched that's where the second part of the plan kicks in.

'Frank will demonstrate his skills with that bow by shooting fire-arrows into the barns. That will flush them out into the open and we can mow them down.' O'Leary looked speculatively towards the creek. 'Hopefully when they see the smoke, your Mexicans will attack. Unless they come on when they hear the shooting. It's a pity I weren't here to instruct them.' He turned back to Catlin and put his hands on her shoulders. 'We'll give them such a thrashing they'll run for their lives and never bother us again.'

He flung one arm wide and his face broke into a broad smile.

'Then we'll rebuild all this again. We can have a first class horse ranch – the best in the territory.'

'Oh, Pa, it's so good to have you back again. I was so worried about you. We'll send Gertrude and Rachel running with their tails between their legs. We can have such a good life here.'

The sight of a racing horse and rider heading for the ranch took their attention.

'If I'm not mistaken that's Marcus,' Catlin said with a slight quiver of apprehension. 'The way he's riding that horse it probably means they're on the way. Well, we're ready for them. Let them come.'

'Marcus?' O'Leary asked.

'Cogan, you remember your old scout, Marcus Cogan.'

'What the hell's Cogan doing here?'

'He's been a staunch friend, Pa. It was him as got you away from Rachel and Gertrude. They'd put a price on your head.'

It was indeed Cogan. He rode into the yard, his horse all lathered up and jumped to the ground almost before the horse had stopped.

'They're coming,' he yelled. 'And there's a helluva lot of them.' He stopped at the sight of O'Leary. 'Howdy, boss. You OK?'

The two men stared at each other for a moment.

'Get your horse away, Hard Hill, or should I say, Cogan?'

Cogan grinned sheepishly. 'I don't care what you call

me, Keane. It's just good to see your old self again.'

'I'm putting you in charge of the outside defences, Cogan. Frank and me will defend the house. When it gets too hot you'll retreat back up to the house. But not afore you put up a stiff resistance. We got a few surprises for those bastards. When we see you coming in we'll cover you from the house.'

'Good to have you back, boss. I'll not let you down.'

Cogan gave a mock salute.

O'Leary replied with a bleak grin, 'Good to have you back, Cogan. I don't think I ever seen you without your whiskers afore. You're an ugly son of a bitch.'

'I reckon we could be kin, you and me, we're so goddamn ugly,' Cogan told him.

O'Leary was already walking towards the house. Impulsively Catlin stepped towards Cogan and kissed him on the cheek.

'Thanks for everything, Marcus.'

Cogan stared bemusedly at Catlin before turning to a group of armed men milling about the barns. He began hustling some of them towards the outer fence. Each man was armed with a rifle. Cogan spaced them out along the fence rails.

'They'll come in across the flat there,' he told them. 'You don't fire until I tell you. I want you to aim at the horses' heads which is about midpoint on a rider. That way you'll either hit the horse or hit the rider, depending on whether your shot goes high or low.'

There was some muttering from the men.

'I ain't shooting at no horses,' one eventually voiced his objections.

Cogan realized his mistake. These men were horse wranglers. They made their living herding and caring for horses. His instruction to aim for the horses was like asking them to murder members of their own family.

'I didn't say aim for the horse,' he corrected. 'I said aim over the horse's head. Now don't worry. You ain't expected to hold them here. When they get close enough, we fire a few volleys to slow them down and then we retreat to the outhouses. Then if they press too heavily we fall back to the house.'

A shout from one of the wranglers drew everyone's attention. The man was pointing out past the fence. There was silence as the men followed the direction of his pointing arm.

'My God!' someone said.

A dark mass of riders could be seen pouring down the hill beyond the meadow.

'Jeez, there's hundreds of the bastards!'

'Don't be stupid,' Cogan bellowed. 'There ain't that many. We've got the advantage of cover. Now get ready. Some of you kneel down and rest your weapons on the middle rail. The rest do the same on the top rail. Whatever feels right. Let them get close. No firing until I give the signal. Make every shot count. They're goddamn cowardly bandits. Show them you ain't afraid and they'll turn tail and run.'

Despite Cogan's best efforts to reassure the defenders, with a few exceptions they looked shaken. They were horse wranglers pure and simple. Fighting off a band of marauding bandits was not what they had signed on for. The oncoming horde of riders looked as if it filled the horizon. Cogan strolled up and down behind the men.

'Remember what I said,' he told them. 'No firing until they are in range. Once we break the charge they'll scatter and run. It'll be a duck shoot.'

As he looked out at the oncoming pack even Cogan did not feel very confident. He jumped onto the fence and climbed as high as he could.

'Come on, you goat-turds,' he yelled. 'We got plenty lead

to send you back to whatever hell you come from.'

As if in response to his words the mass of horsemen began to shift and change. It spread wider and wider across the field of vision. Cogan stared in puzzlement at the oncoming riders. The outer wings of the pack began to curve inwards. Then he knew what the movement meant.

'Goddamn it,' he muttered, 'they're gonna try and surround us. They've got enough manpower to surround the goddamn ranch.'

24

The thundering hoofs of the oncoming force could be heard clearly inside the ranch house, a single storey building of plank construction. O'Leary made a tour through the rooms, ensuring each man was at his post. A brace of defenders, armed with rifles and revolvers, manned every window. On the floor beside them were boxes of cartridges. In one of the rooms was a ladder leading up to the roof. Frank and Catlin stood at the foot of this ladder. They were not talking – just holding hands.

'Better get up there, Frank,' O'Leary called.

Frank nodded at the bandit chief and kissed Catlin on the forehead. She smiled wanly and held him close. Releasing him, he gave her a reassuring grin and climbed the ladder.

His bow and prepared fire-arrows had already been carried up there along with his rifle. He was to lie concealed until O'Leary gave him the signal to start shooting arrows into the kerosene-soaked outbuildings.

Outside was the first line of defence with Marcus Cogan in charge. Striding up and down behind the nervous horse wranglers, Cogan tried to put some backbone into the men waiting by the fence. They were extremely edgy and kept glancing over their shoulders at the buildings behind them. In their minds those barns represented safety and some protection from the oncoming horde. They gripped their weapons and stared with growing anxiety at the horsemen advancing rapidly towards them.

'Remember what I said,' Cogan roared. 'Wait for my signal. We have to wait until they're close. And make every bullet count. When we've put a bunch of them in the dust we'll retreat to the barns.'

But the men were panicky and scared. Someone fired at the distant line of horsemen. Everyone else jerked into action. A volley of rifle-fire erupted from the line of fence posts. Men blazed away indiscriminately.

'Not yet, goddamn it! Not yet!' Cogan raged.

But it was to no avail. The wranglers blazed away at the dark line of hostile riders. It was a wasted effort. The distance was too great. Most of the bullets discharged from the defenders ended up well short of the intended targets.

The oncoming line of horsemen grew wider and wider as the riders spread out. The noise of massed hoofs was like a continuous roll of thunder. It was then the first of the defenders broke and ran for the shelter of the barns.

That one man bolting was the precursor of what was to become a full retreat. In ones and twos the wranglers scrambled away from the fencing and ran for cover. Cogan tried to grab men and haul them back. But no sooner was he busy with one than others fled past him.

'Goddamn you, come back, you lily-livered snakes,' Cogan yelled in frustration.

But once started, the retreat could not be stemmed. Even under Cogan's tongue-lashing they still ran. Cogan turned and stared bleakly out at the approaching horsemen. He began to feel something akin to despair.

'Goddamn it,' he muttered then turned and walked with slow and deliberate pace after the retreating wranglers.

The men were crouching inside the outbuildings, manning doorways and windows. Cogan looked back and saw the raiders very close now. Their strategy became clear as the wings of the horde swung wide of the ranch buildings and they began an encircling movement. Tighter and tighter the noose was drawn.

'Goddamn it,' Cogan yelled at the cowering defenders. 'Start firing. They're close enough now a blind man could hit them from here.'

The wranglers began a desultory defence and did as they were told, firing out at the encircling bandits. Then the riders began to fire back from horseback. Bullets splattered against the walls of the barns. Cogan's wranglers flinched as the barrage began. Some continued to fire back but most were ducking inside the buildings, fearful of the incoming bullets.

'Keep firing, goddamn it!' Cogan yelled.

A man suddenly began screaming and abruptly stood up, blood flowing from a neck wound. Another one was snatched back into the interior of the barn as a bullet hit him in the chest. Around and around the ranch buildings the horde rode, firing a continuous stream of lead into the defending force.

The fire from the outriders was fearsome. A continuous hail of lead poured indiscriminately into the main house and the outbuildings. Bullets ripped and splintered the wooden walls. Men crouched down under the fearsome barrage, unable to lift their heads for fear of being hit.

Slowly the circling riders drew their circuit tighter and tighter. Cogan realized the men under his command were useless against such a sustained rate of fire.

'Goddamn it all, get back to the house,' he yelled. 'You're no more use out here than a chorus line of nuns.'

Men looked at him with fear-glazed eyes. No one moved.

'Go on,' Cogan bawled at them. 'You'll be safe in the house.'

It was a lie he knew, but he realized they were doing no

good where they were. Perhaps in the relative safety of the house the men might gather their courage and start fighting back.

At some stage the outbuildings had to be abandoned as part of O'Leary's strategy. Only when the place was undefended would the attackers venture to take possession and then Frank would shoot his arrows and hopefully set the shacks ablaze, roasting the bandits lured inside them.

'Run! Run!' Cogan yelled. 'Go!'

No one moved. He grabbed the nearest man and pushed him out into the yard. Someone rushed past him and then the yard was filled with fleeing men. The covering fire from the house intensified as the defenders saw the men running for cover. But the firing also increased from the marauding horsemen.

A man screamed and toppled to the ground, blood pumping from a wound in the middle of his back. Another stopped to help. The top of his head disintegrated and his corpse fell on top of the wounded man. No one stopped after that.

The flight became a desperate retreat. Some even dropped their weapons in order to run faster. Cogan was the last to leave the cover of the barns. He ran through a hail of lead. Half a dozen wounded and dead men littered the yard – some calling out for help.

Nobody stopped to assist them. Panic had set in. It was every man for himself. Cogan crashed through the front door. Someone slammed it behind him. He collapsed in the hallway, chest heaving.

'What the hell's going on?' O'Leary bellowed. 'You were supposed to hold.'

Cogan could only nod in acknowledgement, breathless after his dash. He clambered to his feet and ignoring his old boss, ran to a window. Two men were firing and ducking back – firing and taking cover. Cogan stood behind them and fired his rifle at the mass of horses and men. The noose was drawing tighter and tighter. Here and there riderless horses could be seen galloping amongst the raiders, their riders having fallen to the fire from the ranch.

Cogan cursed and emptied his weapon into the encircling riders. The noise was deafening. Smoke filled the rooms. The stench of burnt gunpowder was astringent and choked nasal passages. Some men yelled defiance at the raiders but could not be heard above the crashing noise of firing.

One of the men at the window suddenly slumped against the wall. He slid down, leaving a red smudge on the wood. His companion leaned over to assist him. His mouth moved as he spoke to the wounded man, his voice inaudible amongst all tumult around him. He cartwheeled back against Cogan as two bullets entered the side of his head.

Blood and gore splattered Cogan. He shoved the man aside and crouching down, reloaded. The smell of blood mingled with cordite was strong in his nostrils. He sneezed and resumed firing.

The endless circling along with the firing never ceased. Bullets hammered into the window frame. Splinters erupted from the shattered wood. Cogan did not feel the flake that lodged in his cheek and started a trickle of blood down his face.

Suddenly a group of raiders broke ranks and raced the horses towards the fence. In a few moments they were sheltered from any shooting from the house by the bulk of the outbuildings.

O'Leary stood in a window at the side of the house and fired coolly out into the pack of horses and men.

Aim and fire. Aim and fire.

His rifle was hot to his touch. Such was his rate of fire his weapon jammed. Dropping the useless rifle, he picked up another from the nerveless fingers of a dead wrangler.

Without pausing, he continued to fire with deadly accuracy into the encircling horsemen. He noted the men racing for the cover of the barns.

As he fired, more and more horses were running free as their riders abandoned them and took cover in the out-houses.

'Not yet,' he muttered. 'We need more packed in there.'

The firing went on unabated. Noise and confusion and smell and smoke battering the senses. Dazed men fired with automatic reflexes. Rifles grew hot and jammed. Some took out pistols and used them. Others grabbed weapons from dead or wounded companions and fired and loaded. Some did not even look for targets – just poking the barrel out of the window and letting loose till the hammer fell on an empty shell. Automatically reloading and firing. Reloading and firing.

More and more men were packing into the outbuildings and pouring a deadly hail of fire into the ranch house. Those facing such a barrage were unable to raise a head to fire. They held up a pistol or rifle in the window and fired blindly.

O'Leary finally ran to the bottom of the ladder. A rope dangled from the opening attached to Frank Carter's boot up on the roof. O'Leary yanked hard on this, the pre-arranged signal for the bowman to do his work. The rope was pulled from his hand as Carter acknowledged he was ready. The white haired old man ran back to his post and resumed firing.

On the roof Frank Carter notched his arrow into the bow. The arrow had a wad of oil-soaked cotton bound to the head. A small brazier filled with live coals glowed beside him. He thrust the cotton into the coals and waited until it was well alight. A quick peep over the parapet and then he drew back the bow and loosed the arrow. One by one he fired up the cotton bundles and shot the arrows.

He knew the distances to a fairly accurate degree. But in spite of that he realized some would not find their mark. He could not risk a look to see. After the first few arrows, a hail of bullets splintered the parapet and flew past like hornets. He grinned wryly and continued his deadly work.

25

Sheltering in one of the barns along with a dozen men, Monday eyed the fire arrows arcing into the buildings. Some hit the walls and failing to lodge in the wood, fell to the ground where they smouldered and set fire to oil-soaked rags strategically placed along the base. A few arrows thudded into the rooftops and fired up saturated straw.

'Keep shooting up at that roof,' he yelled. 'We need to kill that son 'a bitch up there firing those arrows.'

He looked around the barn for some means to counter attack. An old buggy caught his eye. For a moment he eyed this and then an idea began to take shape.

'Get that cart over here by the door,' he instructed.

Men moved to do his bidding. Rachel had given the youngster command over her men and they were ready to follow him. Sporadic fire was coming from the house but enough men were firing from the barns to keep the defenders' heads low.

The biggest danger now was the barns catching fire. If men had to abandon the buildings they would suffer many casualties. Already Monday's men were looking apprehensive as smoke billowed into the barn from the fires beginning to flare into life.

'Pile those bales of straw into the wagon. Leave gaps to the front as loopholes.'

When the preparations were completed Monday grinned wolfishly at his companions.

'Right, I need volunteers to man our war-wagon. One man lying in front with me, and a few of you to push us up to the house.'

No one moved. Monday pointed his revolver at a thick-set outlaw with a wiry ginger beard.

'You, I want you in that wagon now.'

The man hesitated, shaking his head. Monday pulled the trigger. The bullet hit the outlaw in the chest. He fell back against the side of the barn. His eyes opened wide as he stared at his killer then he slid to the dirt floor. Monday's gun moved to the next man, a youngster about the same age as the half-breed with the beginnings of a moustache on his upper lip.

'Sure, boss,' he said, and hastily crawled into the wagon.

'Right, I want four men pushing.'

Under the threat of Monday's gun the bandits next in line stepped up and took up the shafts of the cart.

'The rest of you concentrate your fire on that door,' Monday ordered. 'Just keep on blasting at the lock and hinges. When I get to that door I want it to come down quicker than a whore's drawers. I don't suppose I need to tell you when there's a danger of hitting us, you shift your aim and hit that fire-raiser on the roof and anything else you can sight on.'

Monday took an axe from a hook on the wall and put it in the bed of the wagon. Smoke was now billowing thickly into the barn from the conflagration started by the fire arrows.

'Right, what's keeping, you crow bait? And remember.' Monday's cold eyes took on a killing glint. 'Anyone as chickens out on me, I'll personally seek him out and he'll wish he'd died in this here fight.' He paused to let his warning sink in. 'Right, let's go! Get this wagon rolling.'

The reinforced vehicle moved into the yard. The fire-power from the bandits left behind in the outbuildings suddenly increased as Monday's men carried out his instructions and fired a fearsome barrage at the house. The two men lying in the cart held their fire. When they hit the house Monday wanted to go in firing on full cylinders.

Bullets thudded harmlessly into the stout bales piled on the cart. A man cried out and stumbled out from behind the protection of the cart as a stray bullet hit him. Immediately he became the target for the guns firing from the house. Bullets smashed into his body as he stumbled from the cover of the cart. He screamed and tumbled to the ground and still the bullets hammered into his corpse.

'Keep going,' Monday yelled, peering through the loop-hole he had left in the straw bales.

He bared his teeth at his companion in a fierce grimace. The youngster grinned tightly back. The men pushing the cart yelled in terror or bravado but somehow managed to keep the cart moving.

Monday could see the door they were heading for peppered with bullet holes. His main worry was that something would be wedged behind the door to impede his entry. Then they jolted against the step.

Immediately, Monday was up and swinging the axe. The blade bit into the top panel and the wood disintegrated. A boot lashed out beside him as his companion kicked at the door. Wood splintered and Monday threw his shoulder against the barrier.

He found himself tumbling head over heels as the door gave way. Monday hit the floor and rolled sideways as his companion crashed down beside him feet first. Almost immediately the youngster started blasting away with his revolvers. Monday had his guns out and was firing towards the other end of the room.

Three men were turning from a shattered window to fire

144

at the intruders. Monday's guns bucked and flamed and two of the men twisted away as his bullets hit flesh. The third man stood up to fire back and exposed himself to the gunmen in the barn. He suddenly staggered across the room as bullets pulverized his back.

Monday was on his feet now and running towards an inner doorway. The surviving members of the cart team blundered in after him. The young gunman was still on his feet and busy reloading. Monday did likewise. Someone appeared in the doorway and was blasted away by a hail of bullets.

Monday ran to the doorway and putting his pistol outside, emptied it into the corridor. With his other gun at the ready, he flattened himself on the floor and risked a quick peep outside. A bullet hit the doorjamb too high to do any damage.

Monday fired towards the source of the firing. He heard a curse and a door slammed. Taking time to reload, he looked behind him. More of his men from the burning out-houses were scrambling through the broken door.

Jumping out into the corridor, Monday emptied his pistols into the closed door. Remembering the axe, he ran back and collecting it, rushed into the corridor again.

'Follow me!' he yelled.

The half-breed charged down the corridor and drove the blade of the axe into the lock. He immediately dropped flat and bullets burnt the air above him. Behind him a man screamed as he took lead in his guts.

Using the axe like a battering ram, Monday drove the heavy tool at the wood. The door crashed open and he threw the axe ahead of him. He could hear someone scram-bling back. He fired blindly and heard cursing and then he rolled through the opening.

There was a tangle of bodies as men fought to get through a doorway to the left. Monday fired lead into the retreating men and saw one throw up his arms and pitch forward. Another twisted sideways as bullets took his legs from under him. More and more of his men were piling into the room with him. Then Monday noticed the ladder and the open trapdoor. He pointed silently at the ladder and jabbed upwards with his finger. Two men started for the ladder.

Monday paused for a moment. His pulse was racing. He had been so tensed up during the attack he had not time to make plans other than to get his men out of the burning barns and the only way to do that was to gain a foothold in the house. Now he was established he was at a loss as what to do next.

The rooms they had taken were becoming crowded as more and more of the bandits were able to take advantage of the blind spot in the defences to gain entry to the house. There was a flurry of shots from the roof. Everyone watched the trapdoor. A bearded head poked through the opening.

'OK, boss. Son of a bitch won't be setting no more fires.'

'Has he got fire up there?' Monday asked.

'Sure, had a goddamn stove with him.'

'Get it down here.' Monday was all action again. 'Bring in those straw bales.' He was ripping down the curtains. 'Here, pass these up on the roof. They can wrap the fire in those.'

Soon the stove was lowered into the room swathed in the curtains. A busy five minutes later Monday was ready. The oil soaked arrowheads were plunged into the hay bales and then set alight. Monday's men tossed the burning straw through the doorways. Someone in the next room tried to extinguish the fire by kicking at it. His boot became a bloody mass as several bullets shredded it. There was confused shouting within the building. More shots. Monday waited. The shooting eased. Someone was shouting from the house.

'Don't shoot! We surrender.'

Monday grinned.

'Come on.'

Motioning his men forward with his pistol, he leapt through the doorway, both guns blazing. The bales were well alight now and he jumped over them, heedless of the flames.

Frightened faces turned as he fired into a bunch of men gathered by the door that led out into the yard. Behind him, his men followed his example and plunged into the room, firing indiscriminately. The group of men scattered – most hit by flying bullets. Some ran outside and were mown down by the attackers still shooting from the barns.

His guns empty, Monday ran to one of the fallen defenders and snatched up his pistols. He swept the weapons around the room, finding nothing to shoot at. All the defenders were either dead or wounded or had fled out into the death trap of the yard. Slowly he lowered his guns and walked to the front door and crouched down just inside.

'It's Monday here,' he yelled. 'You lot out in the barns stop shooting. We've cleared the house. Come on in.'

Gradually the gunfire petered out. Cautiously Monday poked his head outside and waved at the burning barns. The yard was littered with the dead and dying. Slowly he relaxed.

The half-breed turned back with a wolfish grin to the men who had followed him into the house. His face and clothes were blackened and smoke-grimed from gunpowder flashes and burning straw.

'Looks like we won the day, fellas. Some of you go round the rooms and flush out any stragglers. The rest of you try and put out those fires.'

Among the survivors was the youngster who had lain in the cart with him. Monday motioned him over.

'What's your name, kid?'

'Ed,' the boy said simply.

'I have a special mission for you, Ed. If you come across an old white-haired man and a young woman you make sure they don't come out of this alive.'

For a heartbeat they stared at each other. The youngster touched his revolver to his hat brim.

'I ain't killed no woman afore but I guess it ain't no different than killing a man.'

As the bandits exited the room, Monday walked to an overturned chair and righted it. He began to reload his guns. While he worked he glanced with grim satisfaction at the dead bodies strewn around the room. A figure darkened the doorway. Monday's guns snapped up but he held his fire. Alec stood there with drawn guns, looking around the scene of death.

'Looks like you won your spurs, breed,' he remarked.

26

Alec turned and signalled to someone outside. He holstered his guns and stepped into the room. The gunman's eyes were cold as they stared at Monday. Each man took stock of the other, like fighting cocks sizing up the opposition. A noise from outside distracted them and a woman entered.

'Monday, thank God you're safe.'

Rachel rushed to the youngster's side. She brushed fingers across his grimy face.

'You were so brave,' she told him. 'I'm so proud of you.'

Before Monday could respond another woman stepped inside. It was the leather-clad Gertrude. She looked sourly at the couple.

'Have you no shame, Rachel? Your husband not cold yet and there you are pawing over another man.'

Rachel looked smugly at her sister.

'Only the fittest survive, darling Gertrude. Monday here is a real man and as it is I need a replacement for Cornwell. Jesse was well past it. I got me a young stallion here.' Rachel threw back her head and laughed out loud. 'My, my, sister, have you ate something sour?' she chided. 'Your face . . . your face. . . .'

And Rachel went into peals of laughter. In a few swift steps Gertrude was across the room. Her clenched fist crashed into her sister's face. Rachel's laughter was abruptly cut off. She staggered back, a look of fury distorting her pretty face. With a snarl she launched herself at Gertrude. The leather clad woman tried to fend her off but Rachel's nails racked across her sister's face, leaving a row of red wheals.

'You bitch,' screamed Gertrude and swung again.

Rachel kicked out and hit her sister's knee. Gertrude grunted but her punch caught Rachel on the shoulder. Then the two women closed. For a moment they wrestled together, their shuffling boots and grunts seeming loud to the two men watching.

Monday cast a covert glance at Alec and was disconcerted to realize the blond killer was not watching the bout between the sisters. Alec's cold eyes were fixed on Monday instead. Quickly the youngster swivelled his gaze back to the fight.

Cursing and grunting, the women struggled for dominance. Rachel had her hands buried in Gertrude's black tresses and was yanking so hard that the other woman's neck was arched back. Gertrude in turn was strangling her sister in a vicious choke-grip. The women's faces were contorted in pain and fury.

Red faced, Rachel began to push at her sister. Slowly Gertrude was forced relentlessly back, her leather riding boots gaining no purchase on the wooden floorboards. Rachel nevertheless made steady progress, her face contorted as her lungs were starved of oxygen.

Slowly she pushed her sister towards the doorway until Gertrude's heels caught on the step. With a grunt Gertrude overbalanced and both women fell out into the yard. As they hit the dirt Gertrude lost her grip. The women scrambled apart and gaining their feet, glared angrily at each other.

'I've wanted to rip your eyes out for a long time now,'

hissed Gertrude.

Blood smeared her cheek where her sister's nails had gouged. Rachel, bent over at the waist, was too busy recovering from her strangulation to reply. She suddenly ran at her sister and struck with her shoulder. Gertrude went over, hitting the ground with an audible thump. A weak scream escaped Gertrude as she crashed to the dirt. Rachel jumped astride her and rained punches on her sister. Gertrude twisted from side to side to in a desperate attempt to dislodge her attacker.

Keeping a wary eye on Alec, Monday came to the door and slipped out into the yard. More and more men were coming up, drawn to the spectacle of the O'Leary women brawling. Alec appeared in the doorway to observe the fight with seeming unconcern.

At last Gertrude succeeded in overturning her sister. They rolled a few times, first one on top then the other. As they wrestled in the dirt the women were taking on a ragged and dusty appearance. Grime became matted in Rachel's furs and dust smeared Gertrude's black leather.

'Whaa'hee!' one of the watchers suddenly yelled.

At once the men lost their inhibitions and began to cheer on the wrestlers.

'Go on, gal, smash her face.'

'You can do it.'

'Rip her eyes out.'

'Ten dollars on Rachel.'

'I'll take it.'

'Five dollars on the blonde.'

There were cheers and laughter and betting on the outcome as the women battled it out. At last they broke apart and scrambled upright. Both were winded now. They stood glaring at each other dishevelled and angry.

'You had enough, bitch?'

'Enough! I'll have your head from your shoulders afore

I've had enough, you whore.'

For a few moments while they recovered the women were content to hurl insults. They began to circle, hands clawed as if ready to rip flesh. The men grew silent now.

Alec stepped out from the doorway and watched impassively. Monday, also out in the yard, was watching too but with eyes aglow as he observed the two women fighting over him. For he was in no doubt he was the cause of the rivalry.

Suddenly from inside the house came a close pattern of gunshots. Heads turned instinctively towards the sound. Hands gripped weapons as men looked nervously towards the house. While everyone was so distracted Rachel snatched out her gun. There was a look of triumph in her face as she looked up at her sister. Gertrude began to back away.

'No, Rachel. No, Rachel,' she pleaded as she backed away, her hands held out in front of her. 'This is not the way.'

The crack of the single gunshot seemed a small sound after all the gunfire that had gone before. Gertrude staggered back, a look of disbelief in her face. Her eyes turned towards Alec lounging in the doorway.

'Help me, Alec,' she pleaded.

Rachel was walking towards her sister, the gun held in both hands. The onlookers were scrambling out of the line of fire. Again and again she fired. It was impossible to miss at that range. Gertrude reeled as the bullets struck her. She half turned away then collapsed in the dirt. There was silence as Rachel looked defiantly at Alec. The blond gunman smiled amiably at her.

'Well,' he said laconically, 'that's got rid of your rival for your half-breed lover.'

'What do you mean?'

There was a cold malicious smile on Alec's face.

'Didn't you know her and the breed took a shine to each other?'

'No.' Rachel's face was twisted in disbelief. 'I don't believe you.'

Alec reached inside his vest and extracted some dog-eared envelopes. He tossed them to the dirt yard.

'I found these love letters they been writing to each other.'

Rachel turned tortured eyes to her lover.

'Did you, Monday? Did you ever. . . .'

'Goddamn it, no. I never touched her.'

Alec turned back to the house. He stopped midstride at the sight of the woman in the doorway. Something in the manner of the gunman's sudden checking drew the attention of the people in the yard. All eyes were drawn to the doorway.

Pale and haggard, Catlin was holding a pistol in one hand while her other bloodstained hand was clasped tight against her midriff. A man moved past her into the yard. An audible gasp went up from the watching men. His face and clothes stained with blood, O'Leary appeared like the ghost at the feast. He staggered momentarily and then recovered.

'Hello, Alec . . . Rachel,' he said, his voice just above a whisper. 'They almost managed to kill me. I took out most of them. Catlin here helped. We're wounded some, but still standing.'

Alec shook his head. 'I never wanted your death.' He gestured behind him. 'Your loving daughters ordered that.'

The grin on O'Leary's pale, fleshless face was a frightening sight.

'You always was one to pass the buck, Alec. I'll give you a chance to be a man for once. You wanted me dead and never had the guts to do your own dirty work. Now, if you ain't yellow, grab those guns and do the job yourself.'

The blond killer licked his lips and took a step backwards.

'Kill him!' he shouted to the men gathered behind him. No one moved.

'You're gonna have to do it yourself, Alec. What's the matter? Too scared – scared of a crazed old man?'

The gunman's eyes flicked from side to side like a cornered animal. Sweat was beaded on his forehead. For a moment he stilled and then his hands stabbed downwards. The weapons were clear of the holsters and the barrels were coming level when O'Leary's bullets smashed him back into the dirt. For a moment the body twitched, the boot heels scored the dirt and then the stricken man was still. Behind O'Leary, Catlin slid to a sitting position against the door. The old man turned to her.

'Catlin. Is it bad? Don't you go and die on me.'

Through pain filled eyes, Catlin stared up at her father. Her front was saturated in dark blood.

'Pa, I'm sorry. It hurts real bad. I. . . I don't think I'll make it.'

'Goddamn it, Catlin, don't do this.' O'Leary knelt beside her. 'I need you. We can make this ranch work, you and me. We can do it.' His voice broke as he spoke.

'Tell Frank I love him.'

Catlin's voice was weak and her gaze slid out past her father. Her eyes widened.

'No, Rachel, no.'

O'Leary was turning when the bullets hit him in the side of the head. Brains and blood exploded out from his ruptured skull and splattered on to his daughter. He fell across her legs.

With one last supreme effort Catlin lifted her pistol. Her hand was unsteady as she pulled the trigger. Rachel screamed as the heavy slug punched her backwards. She was feebly trying to raise her own gun when Monday went into action. He fired and the bullets struck Catlin in the face and her features disintegrated. She slumped down alongside her dead father, the gun sliding from her lifeless fingers.

There was silence in the yard as men stared at the scene of carnage. Father and daughter lay together in a grotesque embrace of death. In the yard, the two older daughters lay sprawled in bloody heaps along with Gertrude's husband, Alec. The O'Leary dynasty had come to a final and bloody end.

EPILOGUE

Monday Gallagher was seated in one corner of the saloon behind a green baize table. Anyone familiar with Monday was aware this table was his own personal space. It was here he assessed and valued the stolen goods offered for sale. The town boss dealt out two poker hands, the cards landing neatly on the green table top. Monday placed the deck face down between the two piles of cards.

There was no one else at the table. Monday played alone. As he picked up the cards nearest to him, his dark eyes looked up when he heard the batwings swing open. Out of habit he touched the butt of the colt clipped to the underside of the table as he watched the stranger pause inside the doors and look around.

It was early in the day and there were not many customers. A solitary bartender worked behind the bar sorting bottles and glasses. Spotting Monday, the man ambled across the saloon towards him. From under lowered brows Monday sized up the newcomer.

'You Gallagher?'

'Yep.'

'Was hoping to look you up when I got to California Crossing.'

Monday nodded, not answering. The man before him was horribly scarred. The saloon owner felt a touch of loathing as he observed the disfigured face. The man sat down opposite Monday.

'Maybe we could play cards.'

Monday shrugged. 'Maybe. Depends on the stakes.'

'How's about we play for a Mexican girl and an old man's eyes?'

Monday went very still.

'What?'

'A Mexican girl and an old man's eyes.'

'I don't know what you're talking about. Who are you?'

'I am the fourth horseman of the apocalypse. And his name is death.'

Monday leant back in his chair and let his hands slide over the green baize towards the edge of the table. The bizarre face opposite twisted into a grotesque grin. With that ghastly leer on his face the stranger shoved suddenly at the table. The edge hit Monday in the chest and drove him back against the wall.

The violence and suddenness of the action took Monday completely by surprise. His head thudded against the wall and he felt something give in his chest as the table rammed with brutal strength against him. Before he could recover, hands were reaching for him. Monday felt himself being yanked violently upright. He was dragged across the table, upsetting it in the process. The scarred man flung the dazed saloon owner from him. Monday banged against a table and fell awkwardly to the floor. Weakly he turned his head towards the bar.

'Pete,' he croaked, then realized no help was to be had from that quarter.

An extremely hirsute man was standing beside the barkeep holding a shotgun casually in his hands. The weapon was normally kept under the bar for use in situations just like this one. Looking sheepish, the barkeep stood beside the hairy man and shrugged helplessly at his boss.

Monday turned back to Scarface. The man was reaching

157

under the green baize table and was in the process of pluck-
ing the secret Colt from its hiding place. Holding the gun
by the trigger guard, he walked across to the fallen saloon
owner and helped him to his feet. He pushed the gun into
Monday's belt.

'There you are, Monday. I guess that's what you were
looking for?'

The stranger turned and walked to the bar.

'Whiskey,' he requested.

The barman complied. While the stranger's back was
towards him, Monday looked down at the gun tucked into
his waistband. Then he looked at the hairy man with the
shotgun and let his hands hang by his sides. With the drink
in his hand, Scarface turned back to look at Monday.
Monday noticed the man wore a holstered gun.

'You ready to play fair now, Monday?' the stranger asked.

'Who are you?' Monday asked. 'What do you want? Is it
money you're after?'

'I am the Grim Reaper. I have been to hell, Monday. I
saw a yard filled with the dead and their names were Keane
O'Leary, Catlin O'Leary, Rachel O'Leary, Gertrude
O'Leary, your old, blind father and a beautiful young
Mexican girl called Xaviera.'

The scarred man finished the whiskey and set the glass
back on the bar. He looked across at Monday.

'Before I became death, I was called Alward,' he said.

'What the hell you talking about?' Monday said.

'Alward Gallagher, elder son of Washington Gallagher.
My brother always called me Al.'

'Al? You can't be Al. He's dead.'

The horribly scarred man gave his grotesque smile.

'I am your brother, Al, who was dead. I've come back from
the domain of ghosts to haunt you, my beloved brother.'

The scarred man allowed his hands to hang by his side.
That hideous face leered across at Monday.

'All those dead people are getting impatient, brother. Can't you hear them calling for you?'

'No, you can't be Al. He . . . you don't look nothing like Al.'

'You planted my knife to make Pa think I'd tried to shoot him. Somehow you managed to place the blame on me when you murdered Xaviera. Then you helped Rachel put out Pa's eyes.'

The sacred man shook his head regretfully.

'Unforgivable. As your next of kin I appoint myself judge, jury and executioner. Monday Gallagher, for all those heinous crimes you stand accused of, I declare you guilty. There is only one penalty for such unnatural crimes. Monday Gallagher, unnatural son to a great man, Washington Gallagher, I hereby sentence you to death. As I said afore, I am the executioner as well as the judge and jury. So, it is my intention to send you to hell where Beelzebub, your real father awaits you. You have a choice in all this. I will give you a chance to outdraw me or I'll just shoot you down like a mad dog.'

Monday wiped a sweaty hand across his face. He blinked rapidly. His dark, handsome face had taken on a drawn, haggard look.

'You ain't Al. What's he paying you to kill me? I'll pay you double.'

'What day is it?' the scarred man asked suddenly.

The half-breed looked momentarily puzzled.

'Day? It's Monday.'

'Shall I put that on your tombstone? Monday died of a Monday.'

And Monday made his move. He was lightning fast. So fast he let off a shot before the scarred man had his gun out of his holster. A bottle exploded behind the bar as the bullet hit wide. The scarred man had his gun out. He wore that death's head grin as he pulled the trigger.

Monday got off another shot. It ploughed into the bar. He stepped back a pace and looked down at his chest. A puzzled look came over his face. He began to sway. The gun in his hand drooped. He put his hand to his chest and a crimson stain discoloured his fingers. His legs gave way and he pitched forward on to the floor. For long moments no one moved and no one spoke. The man with the scarred face put up his gun. He turned to the two men behind the bar.

'I'll have another whiskey,' he requested.

The whiskered man broke the shotgun and extracted the shells. He placed the weapon on top of the bar.

'I reckon I'll join you.'

He walked from behind the bar and watched the barkeep serve up the drinks, the bottle rattling against the glasses as his hands shook.

'What'll you do now, Cogan?' Alward Gallagher asked, as he reached for the drink.

'I'm for the gold diggings. Got myself a mule and some equipment.'

Cogan drank up. He reached out a hand to the younger man and they shook.

'Good luck, Al.'

'Good luck, yourself, Marcus. When you strike it rich, you make sure and come back here and spend some of that gold in California Crossing.'

Marcus Cogan walked from the saloon without a backward glance.

Alward sauntered across and stood over to the dead body of his brother.

'I guess you're avenged, Pa. May you rest in peace now.'

He righted the green baize table and the chair and sat down.

'Pete, get rid of that there carcass,' he ordered. 'And fetch me another deck of cards.'